"I was wondering," Edward said.

"Yes?"

"When I come back from Portsmouth, may I call on you?"

"You can visit my family anytime."

"No, I mean *you*, Deborah."

She caught her breath and looked away, staring off toward the open door of the warehouse, where clerks were totaling up a buyer's purchases and accepting payment.

"Deborah?"

"Mm?" Her face was crimson, but she turned toward him and raised her chin until her melting brown eyes looked into his face.

"If you'll permit it, I'd like to come next week to call on you. What do you say?"

She opened her mouth, but nothing came out. Was she wondering what Abigail would say? Or perhaps what her father's reaction would be?

She swallowed and tried again. "I would be delighted."

Edward smiled. "Then I shall look forward to it during my voyage to Portsmouth."

SUSAN PAGE DAVIS and her husband, Jim, have been married thirty years and have six children and four grandchildren. They live in Maine, where they are active in an independent Baptist church. Susan is a homeschooling mother and writer. She has published novels in the historical romance, fantasy, and romantic suspense genres. Visit her Web site at www.susanpagedavis.com.

Books by Susan Page Davis

HEARTSONG PRESENTS
HP607—Protecting Amy
HP692—The Oregon Escort
HP708—The Prisoner's Wife
HP719—Weaving a Future
HP727—Wyoming Hoofbeats

The Castaway's Bride

Susan Page Davis

Heartsong Presents

To my sister Pam, always supportive, never predictable. You were brave enough to sleep alone in the Hired Man's Room for years. You brought us Moon Man and Ambercrombie Benson. Without you we'd all be a little more melancholy and provincial. Sisters forever!

A note from the Author:
I love to hear from my readers! You may correspond with me by writing:

Susan Page Davis
Author Relations
PO Box 721
Uhrichsville, OH 44683

ISBN 978-1-59789-512-5

THE CASTAWAY'S BRIDE

Our mission is to publish and distribute inspirational products offering exceptional value and biblical encouragement to the masses.

PRINTED IN THE U.S.A.

one

Edward Hunter hurried down the gangplank to the wharf, taking a deep breath as he viewed the city before him. In the five years he'd been gone, the docks of Portland had grown more crowded, and they bustled with business. Since the end of the war with England, commerce was good, and merchants in the brand-new state of Maine prospered. So many changes! Maine was no longer part of Massachusetts. What else would he discover today?

When he gained the street, he glanced south toward where his father's shipping company had its offices and docks, but he squared his shoulders and turned inland instead. Abigail first, then home.

As he rounded the corner onto Free Street, he felt the tug of his heart stronger than ever and picked up his pace. At last he would be with her again. His pulse quickened as he thought of Abigail. She'd been so young when he'd left. Had she changed?

He chided himself. Of course she had.

For the last five years, that question had plagued him. His fiancée no doubt believed him dead for most of the time he'd been away. Anything could have happened during that period. She would have matured, which was a good thing. When Edward first approached him, her father had considered her too young at seventeen for an engagement. Several months later, after many evenings spent in the Bowman parlor under the watchful eyes of Abigail's parents, the betrothal had been allowed.

Age would not be a problem now; she must be two and twenty. But how else had she changed? He didn't like to think she had pined for him, grief stricken all this time, but neither did he like to think she might have forgotten him. She could have fallen in love with another man by now. She could even be married.

That thought slowed his steps as he walked up the path to the Bowman house. He had tried to avoid thinking about such possibilities during his years of isolation and loneliness on a desolate island in the Pacific Ocean. In all those lonely days and nights, his worst fear had not been death. He had faced that and come so close it no longer frightened him. What he dreaded most was learning that Abigail had forsaken his memory and married another man.

Edward stood before the door for a moment in silent prayer. *Dear Father in heaven, You alone know what is to come, and You know what is best for me. You saw fit to bring me back from near death in the deep, for what purpose I do not know. But now I trust my future to You, Lord.*

He squared his shoulders and lifted the knocker.

❧

Deborah Bowman broke off her humming as the door knocker's distinct thud resounded through the lower rooms of the house.

"Can you get that, Debbie?" Her mother's voice reached her from the kitchen, where preparation of the evening meal was underway.

"Yes, Mother!" Deborah laid down the stack of linen napkins she'd been distributing on the long walnut dining table and headed into the front hall. It couldn't be Jacob Price, her sister's fiancé. He was due in an hour and a half for dinner, and his business usually kept him until the last minute.

The hymn she had been humming stuck in her mind, and she resumed the melody, tucking an errant strand of hair behind her ear as she crossed the hall. She turned the knob and pulled back the heavy oak door. A tall, slender man stood on the doorstep, taller even than Jacob. Almost as tall as. . .

She stared at his sun-browned face and swallowed the blithe greeting she'd prepared to deliver.

"Ab—" He stopped and frowned as he studied her.

The air Deborah sucked in felt heavy in her lungs. She must be mistaken. Again she surveyed the man's handsome but anxious face. A new scar dipped from the corner of his right eye down and back toward his earlobe, and he was thin almost to the point of gauntness. But his dark hair and eyes, his firm chin, even the tilt of his head were the same. It must be him.

"Edward? It can't be!" Her words were barely audible, but the flickering response in his eyes told her she was not mistaken.

"Not little Deborah!"

Her cheeks burned as she felt blood rushing into her face.

"Yes, it's me. But. . .Edward, how. . . ? You can't. . . . " She gave it up and shook her head.

"It's me." A glint stole into his eyes that assured her he was indeed the Edward Hunter she'd known and admired since childhood. The merry demeanor he'd sported as a youth was replaced by something more grave, but there was no doubt in her mind. Somehow Edward had returned from the dead.

"Praise God!" She seized his hands, then dropped them in a rush of embarrassment and stood aside. "Come in. I can hardly believe it's you. Am I dreaming?"

"If you are, then your mother is baking apple tart in your dreams."

Delight bubbled up inside her, and she grasped his sleeve. "Oh, Edward, do come into the parlor. I'll run up and tell Abby you're here."

"She's. . .she's here, then."

"Yes, of course." Deborah halted, anticipating the shock this revelation would bring her older sister. "I expect she'll need a moment to absorb the news." The thought of Jacob Price danced at the edge of Deborah's mind, and she firmly shoved it into oblivion. Edward was home! He was alive! Nothing else must get in the way of the joy his return brought.

She slipped her hand through the crook of his elbow and guided him across the hall into the snug parlor where her mother received guests.

"There, now. You just wait here."

"Thank you."

His strained smile sent a pang of apprehension through her. She longed to sit down beside him on the sofa and hear his tale, but that privilege belonged to Abigail. The pain and anxiety in his face transferred to her own heart. Should she tell him? No, that obligation, too, belonged to her sister.

There was one thing she, as the hostess greeting him, should ask.

"Your mother?"

"I haven't seen her yet." Edward's mouth tightened. "I heard about Father on the ship I took up here from Boston."

Deborah nodded, feeling tears spring into her eyes as she noted his deep sorrow. "I'm sorry, Edward."

"Thank you."

She took a deep breath. "Sit and relax for a few minutes. I'll tell Abby."

At the parlor door, she paused and looked back. Edward sank into a chair and sat immobile, staring toward the front windows. What was going through his mind? Five years! What had happened to him in that time? And how would his return affect Abigail?

She turned, lifted her skirt, and dashed up the stairs.

"Abby?" She careened to a stop in the doorway to her sister's room. Abigail was brushing her long, golden hair, arranging it just so.

"You shouldn't tear around so, Debbie." Abigail turned her attention back to the mirror.

"Abby, I have something to tell you." Deborah took two

steps into the room. At least her sister was sitting down. "Something's happened."

Abigail's gaze caught hers in the mirror, and her hands stilled, holding a lock of hair out away from her head, with her brush poised to style it.

"Not Father?"

"Oh no, nothing like that. It's good news. Very good."

Abigail laid the brush down and swiveled on her stool to face Deborah. "What is it?"

"It's. . . Oh dear, I'm not sure how to say this."

"Just say it."

Deborah gazed into her sister's eyes, blue and dreamy like their mother's. For such a long time, those eyes had been red rimmed from weeping. But recently Abigail had overcome her grief and taken an interest in life once more. Her family had encouraged her to leave off grieving for the man she'd loved. He was dead and gone, and it was all right for her to go on with her life. That's what they'd all told her.

But what would happen now? Deborah didn't want to be the one to shatter her sister's peaceful world again. She ought to have told Mother first and let her break the news to Abigail.

"Debbie." Abigail rose and stepped toward her, clearly annoyed. "Would you just tell me, please? You're driving me wild."

"All right. It's. . .it's Edward."

"Edward?" Abigail's face went white, and she swayed. Deborah rushed to her side and eased her gently toward the side of her four-poster bed. Abigail sat slowly on the edge, staring off into space, then suddenly jerked around to stare at Deborah. "What about him? Tell me."

"He's. . . Oh, Abby, he's alive."

❧

Edward stood and paced the parlor to the fireplace of granite blocks. Turn. To the wide bay window that fronted the street. Outside was the Bowmans' garden and, beyond it, people passing by, bustling toward home and dinner, no doubt. So ordinary. So common. But to his eyes, painfully odd.

Five years! Dear God, everything is so strange here. How can I come back and pick up my life again?

He jerked away from the scene and paced to the fireplace once more.

He'd left the ship determined that the first woman he set eyes on in five years would be the woman he loved. Of course, he'd seen a few ladies from a distance as he walked from the dock to the Bowman house, but none whom he recognized. The city had grown in his absence, and new houses and businesses crowded the peninsula between the Fore River and Casco Bay.

His thoughts had skimmed over the surface of what he'd seen: a multitude of sailing vessels floating in the harbor, scores of people crowding the streets, freight wagons and carts, hawkers preparing to close business for the evening, and housewives hurrying home to start supper. He'd been thinking only of Abigail.

But the woman who opened the door to him had not been Abigail but her little sister, Deborah. Debbie had grown strangely mature and womanly. She was not the child—with the gawky limbs, bushy dark hair, and big, brown eyes so unlike Abigail's—that Edward recalled. Deborah favored Dr. Bowman's side of the family, no question about that.

She was no longer the awkward tomboy. She had moved with grace as she ushered him to the parlor. Her hair had tempered to a smooth, rich chestnut, neatly confined in an upswept coiffure. Her green gown edged with creamy lace was the attire of a lady, not a rambunctious adolescent.

He turned and walked toward the window once more. Abigail. She was the one he longed to see. His thoughts should be focused on her. It was only the strangeness of seeing Deborah grown up that had pulled his mind in a different direction. He tried, as he had so many times in the past five years, to conjure up the image of Abigail's face: her creamy skin, her golden hair, her blue eyes. He sighed and stopped before the window seat.

He would have sent a letter before him at the first opportunity, but as it turned out, he traveled back to civilization by the fastest means he could find. The ship that rescued him conveyed him directly to Boston, and there he'd found a schooner heading north and east the next day for Portland. No letter could have winged its way to his beloved any faster than he had arrived himself.

Would the shock of his appearance endanger her health? Deborah recovered quickly and welcomed him with joy. Still, Abigail had always been less robust than Debbie. Was he inconsiderate to come here first? Perhaps he should have gone to his mother first and sent advance notice to Abigail, then come round to see her in the evening.

He glanced out the window and saw that the shadows were lengthening. He'd lost his pocket watch four years ago in the roiling storm that shipwrecked him, but he could tell by the angle of the sun that late afternoon had reached the coast of Maine. His gaze roved over the lush trees shielding the house from the street. The full foliage welcomed him like the face of an old friend. How he'd longed for the shade of the maples in his parents' yard during the searing summers of the island, where the seasons were turned about and the hottest time of year was in January and February.

He'd kept meticulous count of the days, as nearly as he could reckon, and consoled himself in the hottest times by recalling the ice and snow of Maine winters. He'd tried to picture what Abigail was doing as he sweltered in exile. Ice-skating with Debbie? Riding to church in her father's sleigh? He would imagine her wearing a fur hat and muff, romping through falling snow.

He walked once more to the fireplace, where he leaned one arm against the mantel.

How would she receive him? What would she say? It seemed

like he had been waiting for hours. What could possibly be keeping her? She ought to be tearing down the stairs and into his arms. Shouldn't she? Edward offered another silent plea for serenity, knowing that the next few minutes would determine the course of his life.

&

"How can I face him, Mother?" Abigail sat on the bed, twisting the ends of her sash between her hands.

Deborah stood by, panting a little after her dash down the back stairs and up again with her mother.

"My dear, think of all he's been through. You must see him. You cannot send him away without hearing his story. Furthermore, you must explain your current state to him."

"Oh, Mother, must I?"

"Yes, I'm afraid you must. Break the news to him gently. He will understand, I'm sure, that you've grieved him properly and moved slowly in pinning your affections elsewhere. Your father and I watched you mourn and weep over that young man for three years. No one can fault you in your devotion to him. But now you've got beyond that."

"But, Mother, it's Edward." Deborah grasped her mother's arm, fighting the unbearable confusion that swirled inside her.

"Well, yes, dear." Her mother glanced at her, then back at Abigail. "Of course we're thrilled that he has returned, but your sister hasn't entered into this betrothal with Jacob lightly. It's not something to cast aside—"

"But she loved Edward first." Deborah saw the agony in her sister's eyes as she spoke and clamped her lips together, determined to say no more on the matter. This was Abigail's dilemma, not hers. Still, she couldn't imagine a better surprise than to learn that Edward, whom she'd always adored, was still alive. Deborah had been only fifteen when the news of Edward's death came, but she had felt her heart would break along with Abby's. He was such a fine young man. Deborah knew that if she ever gave her love to a man, he would be a man much like Edward Hunter.

"Couldn't Father just tell him?" Abigail pleaded.

Mother frowned. "Really, Abby! I sent Elizabeth around to ask your father to come home as soon as he can, but he has no inkling of the situation. And he might not be able to leave his office for some time if there are a lot of patients. You mustn't keep that young man waiting."

Abigail stood and walked with wooden steps toward the looking glass.

"Your face is pale," Mother murmured. "Let me help you freshen up. Debbie—" She turned, and Deborah looked toward her. Mother's usual calm expression had fled, and her agitation was nearly as marked as Abigail's dismay.

"Debbie, go down and tell Elizabeth to take him some—no, wait. Elizabeth's gone to fetch your father. You help your sister finish her hairdo, and I'll go and greet Edward myself and see that he has a glass of cider. Don't be long, now, Abby."

Mother swept from the room, and Deborah approached Abigail's chair.

"Would you like me to pin up the last few locks?"

"Oh, would you?"

Deborah reached for the silver-backed brush. Her gaze met that of her sister in the wall mirror. "Try to smile when you greet him, Abby. You look like a terrified rabbit."

"Oh, Debbie, I'm not sure I want to see Edward."

"That's silly. You'll have to see him sometime. He's home to stay."

Tears escaped the corners of Abigail's eyes and trailed down her cheeks. "But it's been so long. Debbie, I was seventeen when he left."

"I know." Deborah sank to her knees and pulled Abigail into her embrace.

Abby sobbed and squeezed her, then pulled away. "I'll ruin your dress."

"Here." Deborah reached for a muslin handkerchief on the

dressing table and placed it in Abigail's hand.

"If only Mr. Hunter hadn't sent him away," Abigail moaned.

"You know he wanted his son to learn every aspect of the business before he began running it," Deborah said. "Edward was preparing to take over when his father retired. His commission as an officer on the *Egret* was intended to give him the experience he'd need to head a shipping company. The men wouldn't have respected him if he'd never been to sea."

"I know, but he'd been on one voyage with his father already. Why did Mr. Hunter have to send Edward on that horrid voyage to the Pacific?"

Deborah sighed. "Maturity, Abby. Experience. Look at Jacob. He was a lad, too, when the *Egret* left. But now he's a man, and he understands the business perfectly, so he's able—" She stopped and looked into Abigail's stricken face.

"What will happen at Hunter Shipping now? They've given Jacob the place Edward would have had if he'd lived. I mean, if he'd—oh, Debbie, this is too awful, and I'm confused."

"There, now, you can't keep crying. Your eyes will be puffy and bloodshot. And you can't blame Mr. Hunter. The news devastated all of us, and it was his own son who went down with the *Egret* in that brutal storm. Or at least, we all thought he did. Jacob and the other men in his boat survived, and we all praised God for that. You can't hold it against Mr. Hunter for taking his nephew into the office afterward, when he thought his only son was lost."

"Edward's drowning broke his poor father's heart."

"Yes." Deborah picked up the hairbrush and began once more to pull it through Abigail's tresses, then pinned her hair up quickly. "If only Mr. Hunter had lived to see this day."

"He would be so happy," Abigail whispered.

"He certainly would be. There."

Abigail examined her image in the mirror, blotted the traces of tears from her cheeks, and stood.

"I guess it's time."

two

"Edward, what a joy to see you again!" Mrs. Bowman bustled into the parlor, and Edward jumped up.

"Thank you. I'm grateful to be here, ma'am."

She set down the tray she carried, took his hand, and smiled up at him. "Abigail will be right down. She was surprised at the news, of course. You understand."

"Of course." He sat when his hostess sat, perching on the edge of the upholstered chair, and accepted the cold glass of sweet cider she offered him.

"You must have been through a nightmare."

"Yes, ma'am. A very long nightmare." He wondered if he ought to launch into his story or wait until Abigail appeared.

From the hallway, he heard the front door open and close, and his hostess sprang up again. "That must be Dr. Bowman. Will you excuse me just a moment, Edward? I know he'd love to see you."

Edward stood up but said nothing as she hurried from the room. This was getting increasingly chaotic. All he'd wanted was a glimpse of Abigail's face and a moment alone with her, but he should have known he would have to wade through her family first.

The murmur of voices reached him, then Dr. Bowman's deep voice rose in shock and pleasure. "What? You don't mean it!"

Abigail's father strode across the threshold and straight toward him, his hand outstretched in welcome.

"Edward! What a wonderful surprise!" The older man shook his hand with vigor, and Edward eyed him cautiously. He hadn't changed much. Perhaps his hair held a bit more gray. His square face bore the interested expression that inspired confidence in his patients. Edward had always liked the physician but was somewhat intimidated five years earlier, viewing him as his future father-in-law. His persistence and diligent labor in Hunter Shipping's office and warehouse had finally convinced Dr. Bowman that he was acceptable husband material for Abigail. Her father had relented and permitted the engagement just before Edward left on his voyage.

"It's good to see you, sir."

"Sit down." The doctor waved toward his chair, and Edward resumed his seat, more nervous than ever, as Dr. Bowman took a place on the sofa.

Mrs. Bowman, who had entered the room behind her husband, gave Edward a nod and a smile. "You'll excuse me, won't you? I must go and give some instructions about dinner to the hired girl."

"You've moved your practice out of the house, sir?" Edward asked.

"Yes, I've got a small surgery down on Union Street now. Convenient for the patients, and it saves the family the disturbance of all those people coming to the house. The short walk there and back gives me some exercise."

"You look well, sir."

"Thank you. I can't say as much for you." The doctor looked him over with a professional eye, and Edward tried not to fidget.

"So, tell me: What happened to you when the *Egret* foundered? And better yet, what miracle has restored you to us now?"

Edward decided that an abbreviated version of his adventure was in order. He would probably have to tell the story many times in the next few days, but short of Abigail herself, Dr. Bowman might be his most important audience.

"Well, sir, we'd done our trading and were ready to start

home. Almost four years ago it was. We hit bad weather, which is not unusual, but it was a wild gale. The storm buffeted us about, and we lost a great deal of rigging; finally the mainmast went down. The captain could see the ship was lost, and he urged us all to get into the boats."

The doctor placed his elbow on the arm of the sofa and leaned his chin on his hand, watching Edward with his avid dark eyes.

Like Deborah's eyes, Edward thought. *Always searching. Wants to know everything.*

"Your cousin Jacob told us how you had to abandon ship," Dr. Bowman said.

"I heard he survived. I'm thankful for that," Edward said. "Jacob led the first boatload, and they got away from the *Egret* in the yawl. I held the longboat near the ship until the captain came down. He insisted on seeing all the men down first. It was difficult. . . ." He closed his eyes for a moment, remembering the howling wind and the boat lunging on the waves. In his mind he saw young Davy Wilkes leap over the side of the ship and land half in, half out of the longboat, with his thighbone broken.

"Did the captain survive, too, then?"

Edward opened his eyes, shaking off the memory. "At first he did. We had eight of us in the longboat. Jacob had a dozen or more in the yawl."

"Fourteen came home."

"That many? I'm glad. I knew a few drowned in the storm, trying to get into the boats. And we lost four men from the longboat before we reached land."

"Starvation?"

"Lack of water, mostly. One boy died of his injuries, and we lost one man over the side in rough water the first night."

"Jacob told us that after your boats became separated during the night he and his crew sailed on for several days, and then another ship picked them up."

"God be praised," Edward murmured. He had often prayed for his comrades and wondered whether they had escaped death.

A stir in the doorway drew his attention, and he realized that Deborah had returned. As he jumped up, she smiled at him, and again he felt the infectious warmth of her presence.

"Well, girls. About time," Dr. Bowman said.

Edward saw then that another young woman was entering behind Deborah, hanging back as though reluctant to break in on the scene. Her eyes were lowered, but when she glanced up as she came forward, he caught his breath.

"Abigail." His pulse hammered.

Deborah stepped aside, and Edward met Abigail in the middle of the room. She looked him in the eye then, her mouth a tight line and her eyelids swollen.

"Hello, Edward."

He reached for her hands, and she hesitated a moment, then let him take them. She hadn't changed, really, except for the shy, sorrowful air she bore. She was as lovely as he remembered. Thinner, perhaps, and more fragile. She had lost the gaiety he always associated with her. Indeed, Deborah exhibited far more pleasure at his appearance than Abigail did.

"I'm so glad. . . ." She turned away abruptly and pulled a handkerchief from her sleeve. "Forgive me," she sobbed.

Edward cleared his throat. "There's nothing to forgive. I realize this is a shock, my dear."

"There, now, sit down, girls," said their father. "Edward was just telling me how he and several others escaped the shipwreck."

"Do tell us," Deborah begged, guiding Abigail to sit with her on the sofa. Dr. Bowman took another chair, and Edward sat down again. "Your boat also was spared by the storm, then?"

"We drifted for two weeks." Edward glanced at Abigail, who was surreptitiously wiping away a tear.

Mrs. Bowman returned, and in the pause she asked, "Shall I bring tea?"

"Not for me, thank you," Edward said.

"Nor me," said the doctor. "It's too close to dinner."

The young women shook their heads, and she slipped into a chair near her husband.

"Please go on, Edward," his host urged.

"Well, sir, we had a small sail and a rudder, and we steered for the nearest land we knew of. We took on water constantly, and I was sure we would all perish. But finally we fetched up on an island."

"What island?" Dr. Bowman asked.

"A small one west of Chile, sir. Far west. It is called Spring Island after the water available there. It has been charted for many years, but not many go there, as it is off the usual shipping lanes."

"Four years!" Deborah stared at him, her lips parted and her eyes glistening. "You stayed on that remote place for four years?"

He nodded. "Nearly. I hoped we would be rescued soon, but after a few weeks we grew discouraged. We were just too far off course for most ships. The one that finally came had also suffered damage and put in for fresh water and a chance to make some repairs before resuming its voyage."

"The ship that rescued Jacob Price and the others searched for your party," Dr. Bowman said.

"Aye. I expect they did. But we'd gone a long ways before we struck land."

"How many of you were there?" Deborah asked.

"Four of us were left when we first landed. But. . ."

"Some of them died?" the doctor asked softly.

"Yes, sir. Alas, I was alone the last two winters." Edward's throat constricted, and he wished they would not ask him any more questions. Eventually he would have to tell all, but for now he wanted only to forget the island and gaze at Abigail.

She had said nothing since they were seated, and Edward wondered at her reserve. She had never been boisterous, but neither had she cringed from him as she seemed to be doing now. This was not going at all as he had imagined.

He drew a deep breath.

"By God's grace, I was found a few months past and carried home again." He turned toward her father. "I don't mean to be forward, but might I have a word with Abigail, sir?"

Mrs. Bowman looked at her husband, and the doctor stood, smiling.

"Of course. I must change my clothes for dinner. Will you stay and eat with us, Edward?"

Abigail's gaze flew to her father, and her features froze as though she dreaded Edward's response.

Edward hesitated. Abigail was definitely not throwing him any encouragement.

"Thank you, sir, but I must decline. I have yet to see my mother."

"Of course," said Dr. Bowman. "Please convey our respects to her."

"I must go to the kitchen," Mrs. Bowman said. "Do come see us again, Edward."

He watched them go, puzzling over what Mrs. Bowman's words might mean to a man who was engaged to marry her daughter. Deborah was also rising, but Abigail shot out her hand and grabbed her sister's wrist.

"Please stay, won't you, Debbie?"

"Well, I. . ." Deborah glanced at him and back to Abigail. "I need to change my clothes as well."

"Please," Abigail whispered, so low Edward barely heard.

Deborah swallowed hard, tossed him an apologetic glance, and settled once more on the sofa.

Is she afraid of me? Edward wondered. He knew his experience had changed him. He was thin and run-down physically, but his love for Abigail was unscathed. *I must be patient until she realizes I am the same man she loved five years ago.*

Deborah looked hard at her sister. When Abigail did not speak, she said, "Edward, I would like to hear more of your ordeal sometime, if it is not too distressing to speak of it."

He nodded. "Perhaps sometime after I've settled in and gotten used to being home again. It was a time of great testing and hardship. The isolation. . ."

"I'm so sorry you had to go through that." Deborah glanced at her sister again.

Abigail turned her attention on him, but her smile seemed to strain every muscle in her face to the point of pain.

"My dearest," he said quietly, leaning toward her. "I do hope you'll forgive me for speaking so frankly before your sister, but I must know—"

She pushed herself up from the sofa, clapping a hand to her temple.

"I'm sorry, Edward, but I don't feel well. Would you please excuse me?"

Edward leaped to his feet, but before he could reply, she had dashed for the door.

&

"Abby!" Deborah cried, but her sister was gone. Appalled at Abigail's behavior, Deborah turned back to face their guest. "Edward, I'm so sorry. That's not like her."

"She must be ill, indeed." He frowned, staring toward the empty doorway.

Deborah's heart went out to him. The forlorn dismay in his eyes wrenched every tender inclination she possessed.

"I'll go to her." She reached out and squeezed his hands. "Do, please, forgive her abruptness. I'm sure she wouldn't behave so if she were well. Perhaps you could come around again tomorrow."

"Yes, I shall. Please convey my apologies."

"You've nothing to apologize for."

Edward grimaced. "I'm afraid I must, or she wouldn't have

reacted so. I seem to have lost my social graces. It would have been better to take a different approach rather than to shock you all." He took an uncertain step toward the door.

He looked so lost that Deborah gently took his arm and stayed beside him as far as the front door. He had no hat to retrieve, so she reached for the doorknob.

"Do come back tomorrow, Edward."

"Yes, I believe I will." Her heart ached as he turned his troubled eyes toward the stairs, then back to her. "But if Abigail is too ill to see me, you will tell me, won't you?"

"Yes, of course."

"Good. I don't want to be a bother."

His confusion and dejection made Deborah long to blurt out the truth. *Abby's promised to marry your cousin, but we still love you.* No, she couldn't say that. She glanced toward the stairway, wishing her father would appear to take over and tell Edward. Surely they shouldn't let him leave their house in ignorance. The whole town knew. Someone else would tell him. His mother, perhaps. He should not learn it that way.

But their father assumed Abby was doing her duty and explaining the situation to Edward herself. Perhaps Deborah should take him back into the parlor and beg him to wait while she fetched Father downstairs again. No, it was drawing close to dinnertime, and if Edward didn't leave the house soon, he'd still be here when Jacob arrived.

"Good day," Edward murmured. He was outside on the doorstep now.

What could she do? What could she say?

She caught her breath and stifled the words she wanted to shout. They nearly choked her. Instead, she managed to say, "I'm sure Abby will be all right once she gets over the jolt of your appearance. She ought to be able to receive you properly tomorrow."

He nodded and turned away, and she closed the door in misery, certain that she'd done the wrong thing.

Edward walked slowly down the path toward the street. What did this mean? Abigail seemed anything but glad to see him. Her blue eyes had remained downcast during most of their interview, and when she looked up, he saw something like panic harbored in them.

But she was still here at home with her parents. That in itself was an encouragement. His fear that she might have married was unfounded.

Lord, show me how to approach her tomorrow, he prayed silently as he stepped through the gate. *You know my wishes, dear Father, but. . .Your will be done.*

He pulled up suddenly as another man nearly collided with him.

"Sorry." He jerked away, but the man seized his arm and stopped him.

"Edward? Is it you?"

He turned to look at the man. Sudden joy leaped into his heart, and he flung his arms around his cousin.

"Jacob! I'm so glad to see you at last. The Bowmans told me you and your men made it."

Jacob gasped and pulled away from him, his eyes wide in disbelief and his mouth gaping.

"I can't believe it! How can this be?"

Edward laughed, the first merriment he'd felt in a long time.

"It's wonderful to see you."

"But where. . .when. . . ?" Jacob shook his head and stood staring.

"I'm on my way home to see Mother. Come with me," Edward said.

Jacob looked longingly toward the house, then back at him. "I'm afraid I can't. I've a dinner engagement this evening. But perhaps I can get away early. You must tell me everything that's happened to you and the others."

"I'll be at home," Edward said. "We'll have a chance to discuss it soon." He wanted to get away, to have more time to think about his encounter with the Bowman family. And he must get to his mother right away. He'd sent a note to her as soon as the ship docked, but she would not forgive him if he lingered in the street, chatting with his cousin when he ought to be hurrying home to her embrace.

"All right," Jacob agreed. "Were you planning to go by the office tomorrow?"

"I might. Are you working there?"

"Well. . .yes. Listen, if you don't come in tomorrow, I'll come looking for you. I need to hear it all." He lifted the latch of the gate.

"You're going to the Bowmans' for dinner?" Edward asked.

"Well, yes." A flush washed Jacob's cheeks. "I say, Edward, have you been to see Abigail?"

"As a matter of fact, yes."

"Then she told you?"

Edward eyed him for a moment, then cleared his throat.

"Told me what?"

Jacob looked toward the house, then back at him. "Edward, I. . ."

Edward's anxiety mounted to paralyzing torment as he took in Jacob's pale features. Why should his friend and cousin sound remorseful?

"I. . ." Jacob straightened his shoulders. "We all thought you were dead, Edward."

"So I've been told." This was it, then. This was why Abigail felt ill when she saw him.

"Yes, well, it's been a long time."

"Four years since the *Egret* sank."

"Yes. And for the past year—oh, Edward, I didn't mean any disrespect to you or. . .or any presumption, but. . .well, you see, I've been courting Abigail."

three

Deborah knocked softly on the door to Abigail's room. Even through the six panel pine door, she could hear her sister weeping. She opened it a crack and peeked in. Abigail lay facedown on her bed, crying into her pillow.

Deborah tiptoed in and sat on the edge of the bed.

"There, Abby. Don't take on so." She rubbed her sister's heaving shoulders, and the sobs grew quieter.

At last Abigail rolled over, her cheeks crimson and her eyes awash with tears.

"I suppose you think I'm horrible." Abigail sniffed and her mouth twisted into a grimace. "Oh, Debbie, I know I was unkind to him—and I'm sorry—but I just couldn't tell him. How am I supposed to deal with this situation? It's unthinkable."

"No, dear. I'm sure other women must have faced similar problems before."

"I just want to die." Abigail broke out in weeping once more, and Deborah gathered her into her arms.

After several minutes, Abigail leaned back and blew her nose on the clean handkerchief Deborah offered her.

"Look at me! I'm wretched, and Jacob will be here any minute for dinner. Maybe I should stay up here and not eat tonight."

"Don't you dare."

"But what do I say to him?"

"Well, that depends." Deborah sat back and studied her face. "Do you love Jacob?"

"Yes, of course, or else I wouldn't have agreed to marry him."

"And do you still love Edward?"

Her heart sank as Abigail hesitated.

"I'm not sure. I mean, I loved him when he went away, but he seems like a different person now."

"You were only in his presence a short time," Deborah chided. "What changes did you see in him?"

"Well. . ." Abigail smoothed her skirt and frowned. "Besides his looking a bit shaggy, you mean? And that jacket!"

Deborah smiled. "I expect someone cut his hair and found him a razor on the ship, and those were probably borrowed clothes."

"You're right, of course, but I found it disconcerting. Why didn't he go home first and—"

"I expect he didn't want to wait to see you."

Abigail drew a ragged breath. "There's more than that." She seized her sister's hand, her eyes pleading for understanding. "I think I'm a little afraid of him, Debbie. He's not nearly so docile as he was before."

"Docile? Honestly, Abby, I saw great longing and love in his face when you came into the room. He still dotes on you. I dare say he's been dreaming of this reunion for five years."

Abigail sobbed and put the handkerchief to her lips. "I want to do the right thing, but what is the right thing in this case? Though I didn't intend to, I find myself engaged to two men. What sort of hoyden would do that?"

"There, now, don't vex yourself. No one is going to think ill of you. You waited far longer than most women would to set your affections elsewhere. For three years after his disappearance, you mourned Edward. Even then, when Jacob began calling on you, you held him off for a long time. No one can fault you for your conduct on that score."

"Thank you. It means a lot to hear you say that." Abigail squeezed her hand. "But what should I do now? Should I break off my engagement to Jacob, or should I tell Edward things have changed and I am now committed to Jacob? What is the honorable thing to do?"

"I don't know. If it's not clear to you, you must pray and

seek God's will about your dilemma. But I do know one thing."

"What is that?"

"You must tell Jacob tonight, and when Edward comes round tomorrow, you must be honest with him."

"What if he doesn't understand?"

"Did he understand you five years ago?"

"Well, yes, I thought so, but—we were so young, Debbie. Perhaps Father was right to urge Edward and me to put off an engagement until he returned from his voyage."

Deborah's heart twisted. How could Abby consider not marrying Edward now? He was the brightest, finest young man she'd ever known. They'd all mourned his loss with Abby. Yet they'd all felt relief this past year when she'd finally put aside her sorrow and risen from her anguished grief.

Deborah put her hand to her sister's cheek and wiped away a straggling tear. "Pray hard, then, and speak your heart to both men."

A soft rap sounded on the door, and Mother looked in. "Jacob has arrived, girls. Your father is entertaining him in the parlor. You'd best come down and greet him, as dinner will be served shortly."

Abigail stood and inhaled deeply. "I suppose I must go down and tell him that Edward has come back."

Her mother sighed. "You can stop worrying about that. He knows."

"But how—"

"He arrived a bit early, and he learned it when he saw his cousin leaving the house."

"He saw Edward?" Abigail grabbed the bedpost and clung to it.

Concerned that her sister would swoon, Deborah leaped to her side.

"Please, Mother," Abigail wailed. "Let me stay up here. I'm not hungry."

"None of that, now. It's bad enough you seem to have let Edward leave without explaining your situation to him. You mustn't neglect to speak to Jacob."

Deborah slipped her arm around Abigail's waist. "You'll feel better after you discuss it with him. Jacob is a reasonable man."

"Not to mention a very handsome one and devoted to you," her mother added. "Come, now."

During dinner, Deborah sensed that everyone was on edge. After a timid, "You've heard about Edward," from Abigail and Jacob's response that he was indeed aware of the marvelous news, the conversation grew a bit stilted. Deborah ate mechanically as she strove to find topics that would put them all at ease. Her father launched into a story about one of his patients, and the tension subsided.

As soon as the meal was over, Dr. Bowman said, "Jacob, will you join me in my study for coffee?"

"If you don't mind, sir," Jacob replied, "I'd like to speak to Abigail privately." He looked anxiously at his fiancée.

Deborah expected Abigail to find an excuse to decline, but instead, her sister said, "I will take a short stroll with you if Deborah accompanies us."

Her mother frowned. "Are you sure you are up to it, dear? You've had a shock today."

"I—" Abigail glanced at Jacob, then looked down at the linen napkin crumpled in her hand. "I think Mr. Price and I need a chance to discuss today's events."

"You're right," said Dr. Bowman. "With Debbie along, I have no objection. Just see them home early, young man."

"Thank you, sir." Jacob rose and pulled Abigail's chair out for her.

Deborah found the prospect of chaperoning while Abigail bared her heart to her suitor distasteful, but she knew that if she refused, her sister would probably put off clearing the air with Jacob. Resigned to the outing, she fetched her shawl and headed toward the harbor with the couple.

As they walked, Jacob kept to mundane remarks about the weather, not broaching the subject that concerned them all until he found a bench overlooking the water. They sat down, and he reached for Abigail's hand.

"Abigail, dearest," he began.

Deborah turned away and stared studiously at a sloop anchored beyond the cluster of fishing boats nearest the shore. It was not fully dark yet, and other people passed them, ambling peacefully along in the warm June evening.

"I must know how things stand with you and Edward," Jacob continued. "Surely you understand my turmoil. I know you pledged your love to me in good faith, but you also pledged yourself to my cousin. I shan't be able to sleep tonight if I don't know that you still love me and plan to become my wife."

A prolonged silence followed, and Deborah felt Jacob's distress. Even more, she felt Abigail's anguish. Her sister's shoulders began to shake, and the bench quivered. Deborah whirled and put her arms around Abigail.

"Really, Jacob, can't you be more considerate?"

Jacob coughed and stared at Deborah. "Forgive me, but my future is at stake here. Surely I have a right to know where I stand."

"And what about Abby? Hasn't she any rights?" By the shock in Jacob's eyes, Deborah knew she was coming at it a bit strong, but she couldn't help it, seeing her sister crushed by the weight of the decision that lay before her. Suddenly she wondered if her own secret preference for Edward was influencing her to fight so fiercely. Was she more committed to seeing Abigail have time to make a rational decision or for Edward to have time to make his case? She wouldn't think about that now. "Abby has had a severe shock, and a gentleman shouldn't clamor so urgently for answers."

Jacob sat back, his spine rigid against the bench.

Deborah stroked Abigail's hair and whispered, "There, now, dear. You need some time to think everything through and pray about it."

Jacob produced a clean handkerchief. Abigail took it with a murmured, "Thank you," and dabbed at her eyes.

Jacob sat forward, clasping his hands between his knees. He shot a sideways glance at Abigail, and when he caught Deborah's eye, she favored him with a meaningful glare.

He cleared his throat. "I suppose your sister is right, my dear. You are as startled and confused as I am. Would you say that a week is time enough for you to sort out your feelings on the matter?"

Abigail gulped and raised her lashes, meeting his gaze in the twilight. "A week?"

"Yes." Jacob reached for her hand, and Deborah turned away, feeling even more the unwanted companion.

"Abby, dearest, I love you more than life itself. When you grieved for Edward, I admired that. I saw your tender heart and your faithfulness to the man you loved. And I longed for that. I craved to have that devotion turned my way."

Abigail let out a soft sigh. "Oh, Jacob! I do care for you. You know that."

There was a soft smacking sound, and Deborah assumed he was kissing her hands. She turned even farther away, her cheeks flushing, and wished she were anywhere but on that bench.

"Oh, darling," Jacob said, "if your earlier attachment to Edward is stronger, then I suppose you should honor it. It's not in your character to deny it. But in my heart, I can't help hoping you will choose me. Edward is an honorable man, and I love him, too. I promise to hold no bitterness toward you whatever your decision."

"Thank you." Abigail's voice broke, and Deborah foresaw another deluge of tears. She jumped up and faced the startled Jacob.

"I believe it's time we returned to the house, Mr. Price."

"Oh, certainly."

Abigail stood and gathered her cloak about her, and they strolled away from the harbor, back toward the residential neighborhood. Deborah noticed that her sister kept her hand tucked through Jacob's arm as they walked.

They reached the Bowmans' door, and Jacob caressed Abigail's hand before releasing it. "Might I come to call again Sunday, Abby?"

"I. . .well, yes."

He nodded. "I'll see you then. Good night."

Deborah opened the door, and she and Abigail stepped into the hall. She hung up her shawl and turned to face her sister.

"Oh, Debbie, they are both fine men. Whatever shall I do?" Abigail burst into tears again.

❦

"My dear, dear boy!"

Edward submitted to his mother's ferocious embrace. "I love you, Mother. I'm so sorry I wasn't here for you when Father was ill."

She stepped back and devoured him with her eyes. "It was a trial, but your sister was a great comfort to me. The Price family, too. Jacob and his parents helped me with everything, from the burial arrangements to finding new household help when the hired girl left to be married. And Jacob has kept the business running as smoothly as a sleigh on ice. Thanks to him, I have not wanted for money."

"I'm glad he's taken care of you." He noted how her hair had silvered, but her posture was still straight and her movements steady.

He let her lead him into the kitchen and sit him down at the table in the spot where his father always used to sit. All the while, thoughts about Jacob raced through his mind. It seemed his cousin had taken his place in many areas—his career, his duties as a son, and even his role as Abigail's future husband.

He tried to squelch the jealousy that sprang up, forming a crushing weight on his chest. It was only the closeness of the room, he told himself, and the smoke from the fireplace and the cooking smells within the confined space that made him feel ill and claustrophobic.

His mother tied a calico apron over her gray skirt and pulled two kettles away from the fire.

"I hope you were not overset by the news of my return," he said.

She bustled about, filling a plate for him. "It was a shock of the best kind. I fell into my chair when I first opened your note, but Jenny Hapworth was here—she does the housework for me now. She brought me tea and let me dither on. I'm afraid I was overly exuberant for a woman my age."

He smiled and captured her hand as she set the plate before him.

"I should have come to you first."

"No, no, I understood perfectly. You had another errand that couldn't wait." She eyed him closely, her mouth drooping in an anxious frown. "How did you find Miss Bowman?"

"She. . .was a bit more distraught than you and perhaps not so exuberant."

His mother eyed him with compassion, then nodded. "I'm sorry. Well, I set about cooking and airing your room as soon as I got the news. I hope you haven't eaten."

"No, I had a glass of cider while at the Bowmans', but beyond that, I've had nothing since breakfast."

"My poor boy! I hope you still like roast mutton. We've no potatoes left, but there's plenty of biscuits and applesauce and a pudding for after."

He surveyed the plate. "I doubt I shall be able to eat all this. I'm not used to such bounty."

Tears sprang into his mother's eyes, and she ruffled his hair before hurrying to the fireplace to remove a steaming kettle of water.

"Tea or coffee?"

"Coffee, please, if you have it. I spent many evenings in my exile trying to recall the smell and taste of the brew."

He bowed his head and offered a silent prayer of thanks for his food and his homecoming.

The first bite of his mother's biscuit put him in euphoria. The outside was golden brown, the bottom firm, and the top soft and flaky. The inside was pure white and separated into tender layers. The wholesome, nutty flavor answered some craving he'd had for four years. Bread! So simple yet so exotic. During the last two months on shipboard, he'd had hard, crumbling biscuits with traces of mold. He'd gone ashore briefly in Boston a week ago, but the bread in the tavern he'd patronized was almost as dry as the sea biscuit.

He chewed slowly, looking at the hole he had bitten from the side of the biscuit. None of the shipboard food had come close to this. And a platter full of them awaited his pleasure, if he could hold them.

"Don't you want some butter?" Mother asked. She pushed the blue china butter dish closer to him, but he shook his head.

"It's perfect. Perhaps tomorrow or next week I'll put butter on one."

She smiled, and he was glad to see the old look of affection and satisfaction she'd habitually worn when watching her menfolk eat.

"If only your father had lived to see this day."

He searched her eyes and saw that her grief was well banked.

"On the last leg of my trip home, from Boston up to here, the ship's captain told me Father had died."

"I'm sorry you learned it that way."

"Oh, he was good about it. He'd known Father for years. In fact, I had met him before at the warehouse. They'd done business together for a long time. Captain Stebbins, out of Searsport."

"Of course." His mother took the seat beside him. "He's dined in this house."

Edward nodded. "He expressed his condolences to you as well. When did it happen, exactly?"

"Last July. Your father collapsed at the office. Jacob sent for Dr. Bowman right away, but it was too late. His heart, the doctor said."

"I'm so sorry. If I could have done anything to get word to you, I would have."

"Of course you would. Your father was crushed when we heard that you were dead. We both were, if the truth be told. Jacob came to visit us as soon as he returned home from the voyage and shared his memories of the time he had on shipboard with you before the storm."

Edward nodded. "We got along well. I was glad Jacob was on the ship. We spoke many times of how things would be when we came home. But we thought we'd sail back to Portland together on the *Egret* with a huge profit for Hunter Shipping."

"I. . .blamed your father for sending our only son off on a long voyage like that." She reached toward him quickly. "Please don't despise me."

"I never could, Mother."

"I admit that when we got news of your death, I was bitter toward him at first. But after a while, we worked through our sorrow, and I asked your father to forgive me. He was always a generous person, and so, of course, he did."

He patted her hand. "That's like Father. Your reaction was natural, I'm sure."

She rose and refilled his coffee, and he sipped it, savoring the rich flavor. "Mother, I've been told that Jacob is running the company now."

"Well, Mr. Daniels is still there. He heads the accounting department. Has three clerks under him. And your uncle Felix runs the warehouse. But yes, Jacob has been invaluable to Hunter Shipping."

Edward nodded. "I'm glad he was there."

"When your father died, he helped make a smooth transition in the management of the company." She sat down opposite him and held his gaze. "You see, we believed you were dead, son, so your father took Jacob into the office and mentored him in the trade. He'd decided to let Jacob take over the company when he was too old to run it anymore. Felix Price was agreeable, and it seemed the best your father could do since his only son was gone."

"I understand." Edward took another sip.

"But then, just over a year ago, your father's heart gave out and he died. No one expected him to go so soon." She blinked at tears, and her voice trembled. "He was only fifty."

"So. . .what is the status of the company now?"

She sniffed and went on with a steadier voice. "Your father signed paperwork before his death, allowing me to own it. I'll be honest with you: I encouraged him to leave it to Jacob with the provision of a lifetime allowance for me. But your father wouldn't hear of it. He had the papers drawn up all legal about three years ago, after we'd given up hope you would ever be found. He told me that when he was gone I could do as I wished, but he wanted to keep the company in the Hunter name while he lived."

"And you didn't change that after he died?"

"No. I do respect Jacob, but somehow I just couldn't do it. I kept putting it off and thinking I'd take care of the transfer a little later."

"I'm surprised you were allowed to own the business."

"Well, your father made sure it was all legal. He left 10 percent to Jacob, and 5 percent to Mr. Daniels. He's been a good and faithful employee for more than forty years."

"And you hold the rest?"

"Yes, but I shall transfer it to you tomorrow. You must take me around to the office, and we'll see about the papers. There's a lawyer in town now. If you think it best, we can ask him to draw them up."

"There's no rush, Mother."

"Yes, there is. I want things as they should be. I know it has irked Mr. Daniels that technically I have the final say in business decisions. He and Jacob have to come here and tell me everything they plan to do before they can execute an idea. Jacob has been very courteous. Well, they both have, but it's been awkward."

"I'm not sure I'm qualified—"

"Now, don't start that, Edward."

"But I didn't finish the training my father sent me to undertake."

"Nonsense. You've always had a good head for business. You spent years in the office with your father before you went away. You practically apprenticed in the warehouse. You'll take your proper place in this company. Period."

Edward managed a smile. "All right, Mother. I shall do my best and pray that you won't regret your decision."

"Now tell me about Abigail. You said you saw her this evening."

He sat back and drew a deep breath.

"Yes, I saw the whole family."

"And what did she tell you? Did you know that she was affianced to Jacob when you saw her?"

He bit his upper lip and picked up his spoon. "No. But I learned it soon after."

"I assume you want to claim your right as her betrothed. What did she say?"

"She didn't say much of anything. I believe she was in shock."

His mother clucked in disapproval.

"I shouldn't have gone there today." He sighed and put his hand to his forehead. "I ought to have come directly here and sent word there, instead of the other way around. Then she would have had time to compose herself."

"Was it very awful?"

"Frustrating. I had to give her father an account of my whereabouts for the last four years, since the *Egret* sank."

"That's a tale I want to hear soon but not tonight," his mother said.

"It's soon told. I was on a small, isolated isle in the Pacific. Dr. Bowman found it fascinating. And Deborah!" He looked up at her and smiled involuntarily. "I was overcome by the change in her. She was just a child when I left, but now she's—"

"A woman."

"Yes, indeed."

His mother nodded. "A stunning woman, though I don't believe she knows it yet. One of these sailor boys will steal her heart soon, I'll warrant."

"Oh, I doubt Dr. Bowman would allow a common sailor to call on her. He would have to be a boatswain, at least."

"Or a second mate?"

Edward chuckled. Second mate had been his rank on the *Egret*. "Ah, well, a captain wouldn't be too good for her. She's very outspoken. Not at all pretentious, but with a bearing that's almost regal. In the best sense of the word, of course."

His mother said nothing but got up to serve the dried plum pudding.

four

The next morning, Edward walked to the graveyard near the church, accompanied by his mother. She had given away most of his old clothing, but she'd kept a few things that had belonged to his father. He wore a hat that he'd often seen his father wear and a suit that hung on him.

"You'll need to have some new shirts and drawers," his mother murmured. "Perhaps I can find some muslin and linen this afternoon."

Edward felt the blood rush to his cheeks. She was his mother, but still. One thing it would never be proper to discuss with her was his island wardrobe. Hearing her plan what he would wear for linens and woolens here in Maine would be embarrassing enough.

"Don't overdo, Mother. I'm not used to a large wardrobe."

"I'll have Jenny help me. You'll be going to the office and meeting lots of businessmen. You look as peaked as a crow's beak, and you can't impress clients if you're wearing clothes two sizes too large. Perhaps I can take in that suit, but that black wool is too hot for summer. It will do in the fall, but you must have something decent to wear now."

Edward didn't argue. It was just nine in the morning and only mid-June, but already the sun beat down on them, making him sweat beneath the layers of wool and linen. He'd supposed the northern climate would seem cool and refreshing to him after years in the tropical sun, but already he was finding the summer uncomfortably warm. Besides, his mother would undertake assembling a new wardrobe for him whether he liked it or not.

He opened the gate to the churchyard, and they walked

between the monuments, mostly flat slabs of slate or granite standing in the turf. Each of the families associated with this church had an area where their dead were buried. Some had one large family marker with smaller stones delineating the individual graves.

The Hunter family plot was dominated by a big, rectangular granite stone. Several generations were buried near it, from the first Hunters who had settled in colonial times to the most recently departed. Deep purple violets grew at the foot of the stone in a hardy bunch, and the name HUNTER was deeply graven on it.

His mother led him beyond the older graves to a marker that read JEREMIAH HUNTER, 1769–1819, BELOVED HUSBAND AND FATHER.

His father's grave. Edward bowed his head for a moment in silent anguish, then stepped closer. His heart lurched as his gaze caught the line chiseled lower on the granite slab.

EDWARD HUNTER, 1796–1816, PRECIOUS SON.

He gulped for air and felt his mother's strong hand grasp his elbow.

"Are you all right, son?"

"Yes. It's. . .a bit unnerving to see my own name there with Father's."

"I'm sorry. I had that done after your father died, in memory of you. There's nothing buried there for you, of course. I can ask the stonecutter to chip it off."

"No, just leave it, and someday someone can change it to the proper date."

Edward took off his hat and fell to his knees. He placed his hand over the letters that formed his father's name. *Dear Lord, thank You for the parents You gave me. Help me to live up to their dreams.*

❧

Edward took his mother home and left her in the care of Jenny, the hired girl. In the short time he had been home, he had learned that Jenny expected to be married at harvesttime, and his mother would once more have to find and break in new household help. Already she was putting the word out at church and throughout her social circle. Edward doubted it would take her long to find another maid. His mother was not demanding, and the chores of the small household wouldn't overtax a woman.

He was glad she had the sturdy house his grandfather had built. It was not as grand as some built by sea captains and shipping magnates, but it was comfortable. The two-story building was sided with pine clapboards, and two masonry chimneys flanked the small observation deck on top. Like many a seafaring man, Edward's grandfather had spent much time watching the harbor, and Grandmother was often found on the deck, gazing out toward Casco Bay when the captain was at sea.

Edward walked toward the shipping company's headquarters near the docks. When he was a block from the building, a chandler paused in unloading a pile of merchandise and stared at him.

"Edward Hunter. Is it you, lad, or am I seeing a ghost?"

Edward laughed. "It's me, Simeon. I've returned from the sea."

"But I attended your funeral several years past. You can't say nay to that."

"Yes, I've been told I was mourned and missed, but as you see, I was never buried."

A small crowd gathered as more men heard the news or came to see what the ruckus was about.

"Please excuse me," Edward said. "I'm glad to see you all again, but I've business to attend to at Hunter Shipping."

He pushed through the knot of onlookers, greeting the men he recognized, shaking a few hands, and murmuring, "Thank you so much. Good to be back."

The company's offices were on the far side of the warehouse, and he entered through the loading door, then stopped to sniff the air. Tea, lumber, tar, molasses, apples, and cinnamon. Now he was really home.

"Mr. Edward." One of the men recognized him and stepped toward him, grinning.

Edward smiled and clapped the older man on the shoulder. "Yes, Elijah, it's me."

"Mr. Price told us you was back." The laborer shook his head. " 'Tis a marvel, sir."

"Yes, indeed. Praise God, I'm alive and I'm home. Someday soon, I'll come down to the dock and break bread with you all at nooning and tell you of my adventure."

"You do that, Mr. Edward."

Two other workers stacking bags marked RICE stopped to stare. Edward waved, then turned toward the doorway that led to the offices.

A large man hopped down from a crate and blocked his path.

"Edward, my boy!"

"Uncle Felix!"

Edward submitted to a hug from Jacob's burly father, then pulled away, fighting for breath.

"My son told me last night you were alive and well." Uncle Felix slapped his shoulder and grinned. "A wondrous sight you are."

"Thank you, Uncle. I'm glad to see you're still here and carrying on."

"Oh yes, I'm fine. Fifty-three years old and still strong as an ox. Now, Jacob, he's a different sort than me. Started out down here with me, but you know, he's not made for hauling truck around the docks. He can do it, but he's made for higher things." Uncle Felix touched his temple and nodded. "Your father saw that, he did. Put my boy over in the office clerking, then sent him to sea. And now he's wearing fine clothes and keeping your inheritance safe for you. Don't forget that, boy."

"I won't." Edward eyed his uncle, wondering if he'd just received a warning to take care of his family. Uncle Felix had lived his life as a laborer, first as a fisherman. After he married Ruth Hunter, Edward's father had employed Felix at the warehouse for his sister's sake but had privately opined that Aunt Ruth had married beneath her. Still, love is love, and Father had always managed to get along with his brother-in-law. Ruth was happy to see her husband with a job safe on land.

Felix was a hearty, jovial man and a hard worker. He had risen to the overseer's post on merit, not just because of his marriage to the owner's sister. His wages had allowed him to buy a small clapboard house in the better part of town, and Aunt Ruth was content. Her three daughters had all made respectable marriages and provided the Prices with an assortment of grandchildren.

"Have you seen your sister's new babe?"

"Not yet," Edward said. "I sent Anne a message, and the family's coming to the house this evening."

"Ah, she must be pleased her brother's not drowned and dead."

"I'm sure she is. It's great to see you, Uncle Felix." Edward shook his hand and headed for the office.

"Bring your mother 'round for Sunday dinner!" his uncle called after him.

As Edward left the warehouse and stepped into the outer room where the clerks had their desks, he stopped. Several doors led off the main room, and one of them led to the private office that had long been his father's sanctum when he was owner and head of the company. But now the door stood open, and coming out of that office was his cousin, Jacob Price.

"Edward, I was hoping you'd come down today."

Jacob's greeting seemed a bit stilted, but Edward stepped toward him.

"Thank you. I hope I'm not intruding."

"How could you intrude in your own office?"

Edward said nothing but couldn't help looking beyond Jacob to the open door.

Jacob followed his gaze. "I was gathering up a few papers. You'll want this office, of course. Your father's desk and all." He stopped and pressed his lips together.

Edward glanced around and saw that the nearest clerk, while not looking at them, had paused with his pen hovering above the ledger on his desk, as though waiting to hear what would happen next.

"Could we have a word in private?"

"Of course." Jacob gestured for Edward to precede him into the inner office.

Edward stepped to the threshold and paused, taking a slow, deep breath. Memories of his father deluged him: the double window where his father had often stood looking out over the harbor to see which ships were docking, the shelves of ledgers that held the business records of Hunter Shipping for nearly a hundred years past, the large walnut desk his grandfather had brought from England—it was all just as it had been five years ago when his father had wished him well on the voyage.

He could almost see Father sitting behind the desk, sharpening a quill with his penknife. Displayed on the wall behind the desk were an old sextant and spyglass, mementos of the past captains Hunter, and a large chart of the New England coast.

It was all precisely the way he had remembered it. Except. . .

He turned to face Jacob. "I don't recall that painting over there."

Jacob looked where he nodded. "Oh, yes. The winter landscape. It came on a ship from France, and I liked it. I thought it would look nice in here."

Edward took a few paces closer to examine it. He didn't recognize the artist's name, but the composition attracted him with its subdued purple and blue shadows in the snow. He kept silent, wondering if the painting belonged to Jacob or to Hunter Shipping, and at what cost. That led to the question of what Jacob was receiving as salary. Could the company afford to pay them both?

Jacob closed the door softly and stepped toward him.

"Edward, I want to assure you that if I'd known you had survived I never would have made myself at home in this room."

Edward turned and eyed him once more, searching his face for deceit or malice but finding none.

"You were within your rights. It's my understanding that my father asked you to take on a major role in the firm, as a replacement for me."

Jacob coughed and turned to the window. "It was something of the sort, yes." He shoved his hands into his pockets.

Edward stared at his back. Jacob's broadcloth coat hung perfectly from his shoulders, and his posture was straight. His blond hair curled against his collar, a fashionable length for the merchant class. He looked the part of a shipping magnate. But Jacob's head began to droop, and his shoulders slumped.

Edward walked over to stand beside him and placed his hand on Jacob's shoulder. "I've been told the business is running smoothly."

Jacob's gaze flitted to his face. "Yes, everything's fine. Of course, the company was hit hard when the *Egret* sank with her cargo four years ago, but your father was canny and made some good investments on the next few voyages with the other two ships. And I've been thinking for some time now of purchasing another vessel."

"Funds are available for that?"

"Well, yes. Daniels tells me they are. I've pretty much left the accounts to him, but we seem to be doing all right, Ed. Some of our enterprises are more profitable than others."

"Naturally."

Jacob's eyes picked up the glitter of the sunlight streaming through the window. "It was my thought to buy a ship before fall if profits continued this summer as they've been for the last year or so. Another schooner, perhaps. We purchased a small sloop before your father died that we use in coastal trade, but I think we're ready for another vessel with the tonnage of the *Egret* or larger."

Edward nodded. "I know nothing of the company's state at the moment. I'd appreciate it if you'd tutor me a little."

"Of course. Edward, I hope—" Jacob studied Edward's face with anxious blue eyes. "I hope you'll keep me on."

"I have no intention of turning you out, Jacob. I regret that my return is displacing you to some extent, but I see no reason why we can't work together."

"Are you certain?" Jacob's brow wrinkled, and his mouth held an anxious crook.

He's thinking of Abigail, Edward realized. Would the fact that they both loved the same woman come between them?

He walked to the bookshelves and gently touched the binding on his father's copy of Bowditch's *The American Practical Navigator.*

"We've always gotten on well, Jacob."

"So we have. And I'm delighted that you've returned."

Edward felt a tightness in his throat and gave a gentle cough. "I'm sure we'll work something out so that we can both earn our living here. As I said, you've proven your worth in the company. I have my mother's word on that, and I expect I'll have Mr. Daniels's confirmation soon."

"He'll show you the books, Edward. Anything you want to see. It took awhile for business to pick up after the peace was signed with England in '14, you know. Sometimes money was scarce, but we've pretty well recovered. Your father was pleased with the way our trade was going last year. If his heart had been stronger, he'd be here now to tell you this."

Edward raised one hand to curtail his cousin's words. "I'm sorry, but I'm feeling a bit emotional today, seeing my father's office and all for the first time since. . . ." Edward swallowed hard, then brushed his grief aside, determined to get down to business. "You know, I think I'd benefit by a short tour of the wharf."

"Of course." Jacob hurried toward the door. "We've expanded the store on the wharf, you know."

"Oh? I came in on Richardson's Wharf yesterday, and I didn't get a good look at ours."

"Well, our chandlery is twice as large as it was when you left, and I've leased space on the wharf for several other small shops. I hope you don't mind. Most are one-year leases, and it's good for business. Draws more people to our store."

"I'm sure it's fine, so long as we're doing well in the ships' supplies."

"Last year was our best year ever. And I've worked out a deal with Stephens's Ropewalk. They make us eight sizes of cordage, and we sell all we can get, both here in our store and in the West Indies trade."

"Rope." Edward nodded. "It's a good, sound product." His mind was racing. It seemed the company was doing better than ever under Jacob's supervision. He knew it was partly due to the general economic climate of the day, but it sowed a riot of thoughts and feelings. How could he take over when Jacob was doing so well? But this was still the shipping company his father and grandfather had built. Could he do as well as Jacob was doing? What would it mean to Jacob, financially and socially, if Edward demoted him? And would it make a difference to Abby? Should he base his business decisions on what she and, yes, even her father would think?

"Of course, lumber is still our mainstay," Jacob said. "But we've been shipping a larger variety of goods in the past two years. I'm telling you, Ed, having England off our backs has opened up a lot of new markets."

Edward smiled at his cousin's enthusiasm. "Well, if you have time this morning, why don't you walk over to the wharf with me and point out the improvements? Afterward, perhaps I can sit down with Mr. Daniels and get an overview of the financial end of things."

"I'd be pleased to do that." Jacob reached for the doorknob. "And, Edward, whatever you decide you want me to do for this firm, I'll accept your decision."

"You've worked hard, Jacob. I'm not sure what our course should be yet, but I won't forget that."

Jacob nodded, but his troubled frown told Edward his cousin was not so settled as his words implied. Edward followed him out into the bright June sunlight. The thought was unspoken, but he inferred that, while Jacob might feel obligated to relinquish the management of Hunter Shipping, he would not so willingly give up his claim to Abigail.

❧

"I don't want to see him."

Abigail sat before her dressing table, her back turned to Deborah, stiff and unyielding, while Deborah sat on her sister's bed, attempting to count the stitches in her knitting.

"Let's not go through this again." Deborah turned her knitting at the end of the row. She couldn't knit anything required to fit someone—no stockings or gloves. Her stitches were much too tight, throwing the gauge off. But she could knit mufflers and rectangular coverlets for babies, and she was working on one for Frances Reading, whose husband had been killed in an accident at the distillery on Titcomb's Wharf a month ago. Deborah had bought the softest wool yarn she could find and dyed it a pale yellow with goldenrod. The blanket was turning out surprisingly well.

"You were less than courteous to Edward last night," she reminded Abigail. "Go down and be civil."

"Must I?"

"Oh, Abby, is this simply embarrassment over your behavior last night?" Deborah watched her sister's downcast eyes in the mirror. Getting no answer, she laid her yarn and needles aside and walked over to touch Abigail's shoulder. "It's not like you to be unkind."

Abigail's mouth clenched for an instant. "All right, I'll talk to him, but only if you promise to stay with me. Don't leave me alone with him."

"Why ever not?"

"I don't know. He seemed a bit. . .savage, I thought."

Deborah shook her head. "You're imagining things."

"But he was out there alone for years with nothing but seabirds and wolves."

"Wolves? Who said anything about wolves on his island?"

"Cannibals, then."

"Nonsense. I've always liked Edward and thought you were marrying the finest man on earth. I doubt he lost his good sense during his ordeal, though he was forced to give up many refinements."

Abigail wrinkled her nose at her reflection in the looking glass. "Oh, Debbie, I liked him, too."

"You told me then that you loved him."

"So I did." Abigail sighed. "I was thrilled that he'd noticed me and that he chose me from among all the other girls. But he's been gone so long, and he's changed."

"Give him a chance, dear. Have you made up your mind to marry Jacob? I don't want to see you discard Edward lightly. He's a wonderful man, and he's been through more than we know, though I'm quite sure we can discount wolves and cannibals."

"I know it, and I don't want to crush his spirit. I'm just not sure I can ever recapture the feelings I had for him five years ago."

"Well, he's been waiting fifteen minutes already. I do think you ought to go down without further delay."

"Come with me."

Deborah frowned. "I hate this chaperone business. It's not in my nature."

"Oh yes, I know. You're the free spirit of the family. But I don't wish to be alone with him."

"All right. But you must make a promise in return."

"What?"

"Treat him decently, as you would any nice gentleman caller."

"I'll pretend he's one of Father's friends."

It wasn't quite what Deborah had hoped for, and she laid a hand on her sister's sleeve.

"Well, keep in mind that whichever man you marry, Edward owns the business concern that will support your family."

Abigail's eyes widened. "I'm always civil, I hope."

Deborah scooped her knitting off the coverlet and shoved it into her workbag. She was longing to hear more of Edward's tale and decided to make the most of this encounter. The idea of his fighting for life against nature in a beautiful but terrible setting intrigued her. She hoped that this afternoon he would reveal more of his adventures.

They walked down the oak stairs together, their full skirts swishing. Abigail looked lovely in the pale blue gown that matched her bright eyes. Deborah was certain Edward would appreciate her beauty. Her cheeks were slightly flushed, and her golden hair shimmered. If only she wouldn't leave the room precipitately again.

*

At last Edward heard the sisters coming down the stairs. He jumped up and met them as they entered the parlor. Abigail smiled at him and let him take her hand for a moment. That was an improvement over their meeting last night.

In fact, she seemed much calmer, and she even murmured, "Edward, so kind of you to come this afternoon."

"It's a pleasure. I hope we can come to an understanding about. . .things."

He couldn't help staring at her. She was more beautiful than his most accurate mental images of her. While on the island, he had wondered if his mind exaggerated her charms and if he would be disappointed on his return to find that she was quite plain. But that was foolish. He'd known from the first time he set eyes on her that she was among the fairest of the city.

The blue of her gown enhanced her creamy complexion, and her hair, pulled back in honey-colored waves, enticed him to brush it with his fingertips to see if it were truly as soft as it appeared.

"Hello, Edward."

Deborah stepped forward and held her hand out to him, and he released Abigail's and focused on the younger sister. He noted anew that Deborah had become a well-favored woman, and he smiled at the gawky girl turned graceful beauty. No doubt, most men would find it hard to choose between the two if asked which sister was lovelier.

"What are you grinning at, if I may be so bold?" she asked with a playful smile.

"I'm sorry. I just can't get over the change in you, Debbie— or Miss Deborah, I suppose I ought to call you now."

She waved that comment aside and sat down on the sofa next to Abigail.

"Nonsense. I grew up calling you Edward, and you always called me Debbie. We needn't commence using formalities now."

He laughed. "Thank you. That's a relief."

He settled into his chair greatly eased. Deborah, at least, was willing to see this interview run smoothly, and Abigail seemed to be in a better humor as well. The shock of his survival and return to Maine had dissipated. He hoped she was ready to discuss their future.

When he smiled at Abigail, she tendered a somewhat timid smile in return and clasped her hands in her lap. Her lips parted as though she would speak but then closed again, and she looked away.

"Well, ladies," Edward said, glancing at Deborah and back

to Abigail, "I do apologize for any abruptness, but I think we all know it's important for me to understand your intentions, Abigail."

Abigail's eyes widened, and she turned toward her sister in dismay.

"Dear Edward," Deborah said, patting Abigail's hand, "you are rather forthcoming today. I was hoping, and I'm sure Abby was, too, that you'd tell us a bit more about your travels."

He swallowed hard. So, they were not going to make this simple.

"Deborah, Abigail, please forgive me for being so frank, but surely you can understand my anxiety. I spent some time with my cousin at the wharf this morning, and I must know. . . ." He left his chair and went to his knees at Abigail's side, reaching for her hands. "Dearest Abby, I simply have to know whether or not you still intend to marry me."

five

Abigail pulled back and jerked her hands away, looking frantically to Deborah. Edward saw at once that he'd been too aggressive. He stood and walked to the empty fireplace, leaning on the mantelpiece and mentally flogging himself for being such a dolt.

"Edward," came Deborah's tentative voice, "perhaps we could come at this topic more subtly."

He blinked at her. Deborah was stroking her sister's hand and gazing at him with such an open, accepting smile that he suddenly wanted to do whatever he must to please her.

That wasn't quite right. He ought to strive to please Abigail, no matter what Deborah thought.

He brushed his hair off his brow. His mother had offered to cut it. Perhaps he should take her up on that this evening. It was shorter now than he'd worn it in solitude but was still long enough to annoy him when it fell into his eyes.

"Please sit down," Deborah continued. "I'm sure Abby is willing to discuss the agreement she made last evening with Mr. Price."

Abigail caught her breath and looked down at her hands once more, her face flushing a rich pink. Once again Edward found his gaze flickering from Abigail to Deborah and back. Abigail, the older sister, so self-assured and cordial to him in the past, seemed terrified of him. Deborah, the lively, teasing younger sister, had assumed the role of the placid peacemaker.

He hesitated, then went to his chair and sat facing them, his nerves at the breaking point. Sweat broke out on his forehead and his back. He wasn't used to being confined in layers of clothing, and the tense situation combined with the warm weather had him perspiring profusely.

"I'm sorry," he said. "If you please, Abigail, we shall proceed with the topic at the speed you wish."

"You said. . . . " Abigail's voice quivered, and she began again. "You said you spent the day with Jacob."

"Part of it. I had a tour of the company's wharf with him this morning, looking over the expansion of the store there and some repairs done to the mooring slips. Then Captain Moody hoisted a flag indicating that a ship was entering the harbor."

"We heard the commotion about noon," Deborah said. "Was it one of your ships?"

"No, it was a schooner from Liverpool, docking at Long Wharf. Jacob decided to go down there and see if she'd brought anything we'd want to purchase for our store. I went back to the office and had a session with Mr. Daniels, our chief accountant. Jacob had told him this morning that I was back, and he had the books all laid out for me to examine."

"And were things in order?" Abigail asked.

"Well, I've only had time to give the ledgers a cursory look at this point, but yes, I'd say Hunter Shipping has been under good management these last few years." He wondered suddenly if Abigail thought he might doubt Jacob's capability, and he knew that, whether she chose to marry him or not, he must put that question to rest. "Of course, my father ran things right up until his death last year, but since then, all indications are that Jacob and Mr. Daniels have done a fine job."

She nodded and lowered her eyes. He decided to leave it at that, though one small item he'd noticed during his quick glance at the books had prompted him to make a decision. He would go through all the financial records thoroughly, especially those of the last year, as soon as he had the opportunity.

"It must have been an emotional day for you," Deborah said.

Edward nodded. "Yes. Seeing all of the fellows I used to work beside, and of course noticing that some I used to work with are missing."

"Will you go to sea again?"

He paused, wondering just how to answer that question. Abigail also seemed to take an avid interest.

"I might. I'm not angry at the sea. God determines if a man will be safe or not, whether he's walking a cobbled street or an oaken deck. But if I were a married man, I doubt I would make another long voyage. Perhaps I would sail as far as the Caribbean if the business required it, but I wouldn't want to. . . be away from my family longer than that."

Abigail flushed once more, and he felt the blood rush to his own cheeks. Perhaps a change of subject was in order.

"I saw Henry Mitchell in the warehouse today. When I left, he was only a boy. Twelve years old then, he told me. Now he's a laborer for Hunter Shipping."

"His father was one of those who didn't return from the *Egret*'s voyage," Deborah said.

Edward nodded and bowed his head for a moment. "I know. Amos Mitchell was in the longboat with me and the others. But he. . .didn't survive our journey to the island."

"I'm sorry," Deborah said. "That must have been a terrible time."

"It was. We started out with eight, but only four of us made it ashore; Captain Trowbridge died soon after. He's buried there." Edward ran a hand through his hair. "I must go around to see his widow soon."

"Mrs. Trowbridge seemed despondent at first," Deborah said. "She knew one day her husband wouldn't return from a voyage, she said. But after the first year, she regained her vim. Her daughter Prudy and her family live with her in the big house now."

A sudden thought disturbed Edward. "I hope my returning hasn't given anyone false hope for their loved ones."

"No, I'm sure it hasn't."

"I must visit her tomorrow," he said, more to himself than to the ladies. How awful for the captain's wife to resign herself to her husband's death and then, four years later, to hear that one of the men she thought drowned with him had survived. For four years, Edward had lived with his failure to keep Captain Trowbridge alive. He'd respected the man and wished he could have done more to help him, but by the time they reached the island and fresh water, it was too late.

After a moment of heavy silence, Edward wondered if he ought to leave. It seemed every conversation led to depressing memories. He didn't want to throw the household into gloom, but neither did he want to make his exit without learning how Abigail felt toward him.

Deborah shifted and smoothed a ruffle on her skirt. "If you mind my asking, do say so, Edward, but I've been wondering. . . ."

"Yes?" He met her rich brown eyes and saw a twinkle there not unlike the expression she used to don when he teased her.

"Whatever did you eat on that island?"

He laughed. "At first, we thought we'd starve. But there were shellfish, and we caught some other fish. Gideon Bramwell became quite good at killing birds with a slingshot."

"Young Gideon was with you on the island?" Abigail stared at him in surprise.

"Yes, for the first two years. I. . .regret to say that he fell from a cliff while trying to raid a plover's nest for some eggs." He sighed and closed his eyes against the image of the plucky boy's mangled body lying in the surf below. Making a mental note to visit Gideon's mother as well, he strove for a more cheerful note. "We landed there in midsummer, and soon the fruit began to ripen. That was providential. And we found a few roots we could eat, and the leaves of one tree made a passable tea."

"So you weren't starving," Deborah said with a satisfied nod.

"No, although sometimes our rations were short. But as soon as we saw that we had fresh water and could find enough nourishment, we knew we could live there until a ship found us."

Abigail's brow furrowed. "Why did it take them so long?"

"From what I've heard, the first search was arduous but didn't extend to beyond where we'd actually drifted in the storm. They didn't think we could have gotten so far, but we had a sail. After we rode out the gale and had better weather, we made good headway. Even so, we were off the usual shipping routes by several hundred miles. No one would ever go to that island on purpose."

"But it had fresh water," Deborah mused.

"Yes, and that's exactly why the *Gladiator* came there and found me a few months ago. She had run into some corsairs and taken some heavy damage. Afterward, her captain didn't think he could make it to the next port, Santiago. So he consulted his charts for a place to drop anchor, do some repairs, and restock the water supply. I thank God he chose my island."

"But you were alone by then," Deborah said softly.

Edward nodded. "Yes. Captain Trowbridge was feverish when we landed, and he didn't last more than a few days. John Webber, Gideon Bramwell, and I kept each other company for more than a year. Then John cut himself badly while skinning a shark. His wound became infected. We tried everything we thought might help, but he died a few weeks later after much suffering."

"Such a pity," Abigail murmured.

"Yes. And then last year, I lost Gideon." Edward sighed. "That was my darkest hour. I thought I would die there as well, and no one would ever know what became of us. Our struggles in the storm and survival for so long were in vain. I fully expected to meet my end alone on that desolate shore."

"Did you remain in such low spirits for a year?" Deborah asked.

He recalled the turmoil and despair that had racked his heart, and the manner in which God had lifted it. "No. God is good, and He did not forsake me. He brought me another friend."

"A friend?" Abigail asked, and Deborah's eyes glittered with anticipation.

"Aye. His name was Kufu."

Both young women leaned forward, eager to hear his explanation.

"A native man?" Abigail asked.

"No."

"A monkey?" guessed Deborah.

"No, Kufu was a seagull. He arrived with a storm, and from how far he came over the sea, I've no way of knowing. His strength was spent, and he flew into my hut for sanctuary. He startled me, but when I saw that he was about done in, I let him rest and offered him some fish entrails and fruit. Before long, he was eating out of my hand."

"He stayed there with you?" Deborah's eyes lit up in delight.

"Yes. I gave him a name I'd heard a sailor call his parrot once, and Kufu was my constant companion from then until the *Gladiator* came."

"Why didn't you bring him home with you?" Deborah asked.

"Alas, he made the choice. He rode out to the ship with me in her longboat, riding on my shoulder. But once we were aboard and the crew raised anchor, he left me and flew back to the island."

They sat in silence for a moment; then Abigail asked, "Do you miss him?"

"I did at first, but now that I'm home again, I can't help feeling it is for the best. No doubt he will find others of his kind. He's strong again now. He has probably already left the island and flown back to wherever he came from. But I can't help believing God sent him to me when He did as a distraction and an encouragement. You see, Kufu needed me at first, so I fought to live. I had no idea how long I'd remain there."

"Four years," Deborah said.

"Yes. Well, close to that. More than three and a half years on that little piece of earth. And the last year alone, save for

Kufu. But with God's help, I could have stayed there longer if necessary. So long as I remembered His goodness, I was willing to wait."

"That's a remarkable tale," Deborah said.

Abigail nodded. "Thank you for telling us. I. . .feel I understand things a bit better now."

Deborah stood. "Let me bring in some refreshment. I think we could all use a cup of tea."

"Not for me," Edward said quickly.

"Sweet cider, then?" Deborah asked.

"Yes, thank you." That sounded much better than anything hot. Edward leaned back in his chair and watched her bustle out the doorway.

It took him a second to realize that at last he was alone with Abigail.

☙

As Deborah opened the kitchen door, her mother looked up from pouring hot water into her teapot.

"Time for a bit of refreshment in the parlor," Deborah explained.

"You've left them alone?"

Deborah chuckled at her grimace. "Yes, but both were calm when I made my retreat. I hope Abby is sensible enough to use this time to tell Edward what transpired between her and Jacob last night."

"Well, here, you can have this tea."

"No, Edward's feeling the heat, I think, though Abby might welcome a cup. I'll take some cool cider with Edward."

"There's a jug in the washroom."

Deborah opened the back door and stepped down into the cool, earthen-floored room at the rear of the house. Here was where the Bowman women and Elizabeth, the hired girl, did the family's laundry. Dug down into the ground two feet and well shaded, the washroom stayed a bit cooler than the kitchen on hot summer days, and Mrs. Bowman stored her milk and butter here, along with any other foods she wanted to keep cool.

Deborah found a jug of sweet cider nestled between the butter crock and the vinegar jug and carried it back into the kitchen.

"Take some of this gingerbread, too," her mother said. "I'll cut it for you."

Deborah brought dishes and forks to add to her tray. "Be sure to save some for Father."

"I will."

"Father's not home yet?" Deborah asked as she worked.

"No."

"He missed luncheon."

"Yes. He sent Peter round to tell me Mrs. Reading delivered a son, but the doctor was called almost immediately after the birth to the Collins farm, where one of the children met with an accident."

"Oh, dear. I hope it's not serious."

"That is my prayer," Mother said. "Do you suppose Abigail has made up her mind?"

"If so, she hasn't confided in me." Deborah carefully poured two glasses of cider and corked the jug. "I don't mind admitting that I hope she'll choose Edward. He has first claim, after all, and I always found him great fun."

"Hardly a reason to marry a man," her mother said. "Edward's a good lad. He's a hard worker, too. But then, so is Jacob. Your father's come to like Jacob a lot. He's steady."

"Edward's steady."

"Well, he was," she agreed, "but is he still? We don't know, do we?"

"Oh, come now, Mother. You know he was always a true friend and faithful in churchgoing. His father was training him in business, and he always obeyed and treated his parents with respect."

"That's true. They say a man will treat his wife the way he

treats his mother, and I've no complaints about how Mrs. Hunter's son treated her before he. . .went away."

Deborah looked into her worried eyes and smiled. "Awkward, isn't it?"

"Yes, a bit. And if I'm having a hard time coming to terms with his being dead, then alive again, I guess we can't blame Abby for needing some time to settle her mind."

"Well, I have nothing against Jacob. He's a fine man, too. But Edward is different. I always thought he was special."

Her mother shot her an inquisitive glance, and for no reason, Deborah felt her cheeks redden. Her laden tray was ready, and she picked it up and escaped into the hallway. She paused at the open parlor door, hearing Abigail's soft tone.

"And so, I honestly don't know yet what I shall do," she said, a catch in her voice. "It's true I loved you dearly, but it's been a very long time; it's also true that I've developed feelings for your cousin. At first I thought it was wrong, but Mother and Father both assured me it was not sinful to. . .find love again after. . .losing the one I. . ."

She faltered, and Edward's low voice came. "I'm sorry I put you in such distress, Abby."

"I beg you to be patient, Edward, while I seek God's will in the matter."

"I shall," he replied. "And I'll pray for your peace where this is concerned."

"Thank you."

Abigail choked a bit on the words, and Deborah stepped forward. She hated to break in on them, but the weight of the tray was causing her wrists to ache.

When he spied her, Edward leaped up from the sofa where he'd been seated beside Abigail and took the tray from her, setting it on the side table. Deborah noted his grave expression as he looked to her for direction.

"Thank you. Abby, I brought you tea; I hope that's your preference."

She handed Edward his cider and gingerbread and settled back on the sofa with Abigail, placing her own cup and dish close at hand.

"Father's been called out to the Collins place," she announced. "The boy studying medicine with him brought Mother a message. I doubt he'll be home before evening."

Abigail's taut face smoothed into serenity. "Poor Father. He works too hard."

"He thrives on it," Deborah said.

"Your father is a remarkable man." Edward took the chair he'd occupied earlier and sipped his cider, then placed the cup on the table. "Won't you tell me about the folks in the neighborhood? Is Pastor Jordan still at the church?"

For the next half hour, they brought him up to date on the doings of their mutual acquaintances, and Deborah was pleased to see Abigail join in with a few anecdotes. She even laughed once, a musical chuckle, and Edward's eyes sparkled when he heard it.

Deborah longed to learn more about his exile on the distant island, but since she knew reverting to that subject would upset Abigail again, she tucked her questions away. Someday she would have a chance to talk to Edward privately. She had no doubt he would reveal the details of his sojourn to her. But for Abby, the topic was best put aside. Her quiet, well-ordered life had become chaos, and Deborah knew her sister needed time to sort it out.

six

Four days later, Edward felt easier in his new role at Hunter Shipping. The men of the warehouse and docks, along with the sloop's crew, all seemed happy to have a Hunter once more giving the orders. The clerks in the office appeared to be a bit more unsettled by his reappearance, but he'd taken a few minutes to thank each man for his service and assure him that, so long as he continued to do his tasks well, his position was secure. Edward had no intention of making any sweeping changes in the office.

Mr. Daniels brought him the ledgers for the previous year on Monday morning, slipping quietly into the private office and laying them on a shelf near Edward's desk.

"The books you wished to look at, sir."

"Thank you." Edward glanced up from the correspondence he was reviewing. "Mr. Daniels, you saw this letter that came in from the shipwright in Bath?"

"Yes, sir."

"And you think we are in good shape to meet his needs?"

"Oh yes, sir. We've done quite a lot of business with him the last couple of years. Masts and spars for a small trading vessel, he wants, and sails and cordage. Not a worry there, sir."

"Good. And the extra barrels of tar he asked about?"

"We have plenty."

"Excellent. Perhaps we should send the sloop up there this week, then."

Daniels ducked his head. "Very good, Mr. Hunter. Will you speak to Captain Jackson?"

Edward eyed the stack of ledgers on the shelf. That job would be less interesting and more exacting. Still, he needed to do it as soon as possible. He looked up at Daniels.

"Mr. Price can handle that, I think. I'll speak to him if he's in the office."

"I believe he stepped over to the wharf, sir."

Edward nodded. "Then I'll send a note over by one of the clerks. He can tell Captain Jackson to alert his crew and prepare to load the supplies for the shipwright." He reached for a quill and a scrap of paper.

An hour later, he was immersed in the ledgers, flipping back and forth between the accounts. Twice he went to the door and called for Daniels to come and explain an entry to him. The older man seemed a bit amused by his intense interest in the ledgers. Edward had studied accounting only in passing during his office training as a teenager and then only at his father's insistence. He'd been much more eager to get out on the wharf and sail up and down the coast on short trading voyages. But he knew his father had gone over the books closely at the end of each month and had spent several days at the close of each year reconciling all the accounts.

Once again he called Daniels to his side. "Did Mr. Price examine the books this year?"

"Oh no, sir," the older man replied, removing his pince-nez from the bridge of his nose. "Mr. Price is very good with the customers and the sailors, but he's not much for figures. He signs off on the payroll each month, but he's left most other matters in my hands."

Edward frowned. "My father always prepared a summary of the previous year's business in January."

Daniels cleared his throat. "Well, sir, I totaled things up and reported to Mr. Price on the year's income and expenses, and he seemed to think that was sufficient."

Edward wondered. He found nothing amiss as he scrutinized the columns of figures, but something still seemed the slightest bit out of order. He couldn't put his finger on it. Cargoes brought in on the sloop and the two schooners, the

Prosper and the *Falcon*; wares bought from other ships that landed in Portland; goods sold in the chandlery and from the warehouse on market days; wages paid out to the men—the notations seemed endless.

At last he put the ledgers aside. He wondered if he could secure an interview with Abigail tonight. The week she'd told him Jacob had given her to make her decision was scarcely half over, yet he couldn't help feeling she was close to knowing her mind. He'd stopped by the Bowmans' modest brick house for a few minutes last evening, but he'd only had his fears confirmed. She was polite, not encouraging.

On the other hand, if he let her continue thinking it over, would his chances of coming out the victor be any better? His spirits were low, and he realized the shock of having to deal with all the changes at hand weighed heavily on him. He'd expected to come home and find his father here to guide him and Abigail ready to marry him. Instead he was bereft and lonely, and his future seemed bleak. He folded his hands on the top of the glossy walnut desk and bowed his head to pray.

He felt better when he had once again committed his future to God. Rising from the desk, he decided to amble across the street to the wharf and see if he could find Jacob.

Edward had spent the weekend visiting with his family. His sister, Anne, and her family had driven up from Saco in their farm wagon and spent a night at the Hunter house. Edward had made the acquaintance of his two-year-old nephew and Anne's new daughter, a babe of three months. On Sunday, they had all taken dinner with Aunt Ruth and Uncle Felix Price. Jacob had excused himself shortly after the meal, and Edward had no doubt he headed to Doctor Bowman's residence. Perhaps it was time to speak openly about Abigail.

Edward didn't want to avoid his cousin. They worked at the same business, and he couldn't see any sense in not speaking to each other. So far they had kept any necessary communication brief. But Edward's hopes of being welcomed into the Bowman family circle decreased with each day, and there was no sense in not acknowledging that.

He found his cousin at the chandlery, helping the man who managed the store for them. The chandlery specialized in ships' supplies, and several of the warehouse laborers were carrying goods from the store out to the sloop.

"Jacob, could I speak to you?"

"Of course." Jacob handed the list to the chandler and followed Edward outside. The wind whipped their coats and the rigging of the sloop that lay secured at the side of the wharf. Edward took Jacob around the corner and into the lee of the building, letting it shelter them.

"What is it?" Jacob asked.

Edward sighed and leaned on a piling, looking off toward the next wharf. A brig was docked, and men scrambled over her decks, laying in supplies by the look of things. "We need to find room for an office for you."

"I'm getting along fine."

"No, you're not. I saw you bending over the apprentice clerk's desk to work on an order yesterday. You need your own desk and space to lay out your work. I've displaced you."

"Edward, there's no need—"

"I say there is." He turned to face Jacob. "You're a 10 percent partner in this company, and a valued member here. You're much better at some aspects of the business than I am. There's no reason we can't work together. We'll partition off some space at the end of the front room. It won't be as large as my office, but I daresay we can make you comfortable."

Jacob pursed his lips for a moment, studying Edward's face. "I won't say no to that proposal."

"Good. That's one thing we agree on."

"What do you mean by that?" Jacob leaned forward, frowning. "Ed, we've been friends since childhood, not to mention our blood ties. Can't we be frank with one another?"

"Yes, of course." Edward walked over to a stack of crates

piled against the back wall of the store and sat down. Jacob hesitated a moment, then joined him.

"You want honesty?" Edward asked. "All right, I'm getting tired of this game we're playing with Abigail, and I expect you are, too."

Jacob ran a finger around the inside of his collar, not meeting Edward's gaze. "Well, cousin, you know she's promised to give me her decision by Friday."

"Yes, well, we both know what she's going to say, don't we?"

"Do we?" Jacob stared at him, an open challenge charging the air between them.

Edward jumped up and strode to the edge of the pier. He shoved his hands into his pockets and stood still for a moment, then exhaled deeply. "This is difficult for me, but I've got to face facts. She loves you. She no longer. . ."

He clamped his lips together and stared out at the waves troubling the harbor. "She no longer feels about me the way she did five years ago. That much is obvious to me."

He heard Jacob's footsteps and knew he had come to stand just behind him.

"Edward, I never. . . Please, you've got to know I didn't intend to spoil anything for you."

"I know, I know." Edward swung around and forced a smile. The pain he had expected wasn't in his heart. Instead, he felt chagrin. Jacob's face bore a bulldoggish look that Edward had often seen Uncle Felix wear.

"I've seen it coming," Edward said. "I just didn't want to admit it. She loves you. And you'd better love her as much or more, because if I find out you don't. . ."

Jacob's lips drew back, and his brows lowered in a good-natured wince. He extended his hand, and Edward shook it.

"I love her," Jacob assured him. "I would do anything for her. You know I love sailing, but I shall never sail again unless it's a short hop up the coast on business. No more voyaging for me."

"That seems extreme."

"It's not. I'll never do to her what you did. Oh, I'm not blaming you for getting shipwrecked—it could as easily have been me on that island. But knowing Abigail as I do now, I can see that the mere prospect of me not returning from a voyage would kill her. I'm staying ashore for the rest of my life, Ed. For her sake."

"Does she know that?"

"Yes."

Edward drew in a deep breath. *Dear Lord, should I just give up altogether? If I promised to stay on land, would she change her mind? Should I even attempt to find out? God, give me wisdom.*

He walked once more to the edge of the wharf and leaned on the piling.

"I think Deborah is getting tired of it, too. Last night she made no secret she despises chaperoning her sister."

Jacob laughed. "Yes, she made her father supervise Abby and me on Sunday. But if Abby affirms that I'm her choice, I should get more private time with her soon."

Edward nodded and managed a feeble smile. His disappointment ached in his heart with a dull, constant throb. *So be it, Father in heaven. Give me Your peace, and bless their union.*

&

"I've made up my mind," Abigail announced at breakfast the next morning.

Deborah's stomach twisted, and she laid down her fork.

"About time," her father said, not looking up from his copy of the *Eastern Herald*.

Mother was more sympathetic. "And which young man can we anticipate becoming our son-in-law?"

"Jacob, of course," Deborah muttered.

"You needn't scowl at me." Abigail broke a small piece of crust off her toast and tossed the morsel across the table, hitting Deborah's shoulder.

"Abby!" their mother scolded.

Abigail turned back to her mother. "Deborah thinks she knows what is best for me, but this is something I must decide for myself."

Deborah felt the accusation was somewhat unjust. It was true she had hoped her sister would choose Edward, but she had never tried to persuade Abigail to do so.

"I haven't attempted to influence your decision."

"Haven't you? You're always telling me how fine and upstanding Edward is."

"I just think you need to consider all aspects of the two gentlemen's characters."

"I have," Abigail said. "And I have made up my mind. Both are admirable, but Jacob is more. . .civilized."

"That's ridiculous."

"Here, now," their father interrupted. "You sound like a gaggle of geese fighting over a handful of corn, not two genteel ladies."

Deborah sank lower in her chair. It wasn't easy to disturb her father's placid nature. Abigail's turmoil must have bothered him these past few days, no matter how calm he appeared.

"And when will you tell the favored gentleman?" their mother asked, smiling. Deborah imagined that in her mind she had already resumed the wedding plans interrupted so rudely a week ago.

"This evening. And I've asked Edward to come by this afternoon if he can get away from the office long enough." Abigail glanced at Deborah. "I thought I should give him a private audience before my renewed betrothal to Jacob becomes public."

It was less than Deborah had hoped for, but more than she'd feared.

"Do treat him gently. He's loved you for such a long time, Abby." Annoyed with her own tender emotions, Deborah blinked rapidly and succeeded in keeping back tears.

"I shall. Of course, you understand that when I say 'private,'

I mean that you shall be present as a chaperone."

"Never."

"What?" Abigail's rosebud mouth hung open.

Before her sister could wail to their mother for support, Deborah said, "I've sat by and listened to both these poor men lay their hearts at your feet. I do not wish to be present when you dash Edward's hopes."

"But—"

"Surely you can do this one thing on your own."

Abigail frowned. "Perhaps Father will tell him for me. I could send him around to your surgery, Father."

The newspaper shivered, and a deep, foreboding voice came from behind it. "I shall do no such thing."

Abigail looked to the other end of the table.

"Nor I," said her mother.

Tears streamed down Abigail's cheeks. "You all think I'm horrid, don't you?"

"No." Her mother rose and began to stack the dishes. "Jacob is a splendid young man, and we shall be proud to have him in the family. But you must do your own work with Edward, Abby. Don't send him away thinking you are a coward."

Abigail inhaled and looked at Deborah.

Deborah tried not to return her gaze, but the sound of Abby's shaky breath pierced her armor.

"Please?" Abigail whispered.

Deborah threw down her napkin.

"All right, but this is the last time. I mean the *last*. Don't come looking for me tonight. I intend to be far away when Jacob reaps the reward of his persistence."

"Thank you, dear sister."

Deborah stamped her foot. "Abby, you aggravate me so. If I ever ask you to chaperone me, please remind me of this moment and say no."

"In order for that to happen, you must stop ignoring all the young men who hover around you after church every Sunday."

Abigail's watery smile was as exasperating as her comment.

As Deborah stomped from the room, she glanced at her father, not trying to suppress the resentment she felt. Hiding behind that newspaper! He ought to have interfered. Sometimes she thought he used his medical practice as an excuse to avoid the feminine intrigues that seethed at home.

She was startled when his complacent voice came once more. "Perhaps she will do that when she finds one who matches the young man she's been defending so passionately."

Deborah stopped even with his chair and stared at him.

As he folded his newspaper precisely, his eyes turned her way, and he threw her a conspiratorial wink.

seven

For once, Abigail was waiting in the parlor before her guest arrived. She sat on the sofa, twisting her handkerchief.

Deborah stood at the window, watching for Edward. The sooner this was over with, the better.

"Do you hate me?"

Deborah sighed and let the sheer curtain fall back into place. "No. But I shall be disgusted with you if you're not frank and to the point with him."

"I'll try."

"Oh, Abby, pretend you are Father doing surgery. This is a necessary procedure. Make it clean and quick, will you?" She plopped down on one of the velvet-covered side chairs.

"Do you think he knows why I've invited him here?"

"Of course."

Abigail's eyes widened in surprise. "Really? Oh dear."

Deborah threw her hands up in resignation. "You love Jacob. That settles it. It would be wrong for you to accept Edward now. You can't marry a man you don't love."

"Well, yes." Abigail wiped an errant tear from her cheek. "So. . .you think it's all right?"

Deborah was glad her sister could not see the chaos in her heart at that moment. "I know you've thrashed this out with God."

"Yes, I have."

"Are you at peace with your decision?"

"I am."

Deborah moved to the sofa and slipped her arm around Abigail's shoulders. "Then this is right. Thank God, and carry it through."

Abigail squeezed her in a suffocating embrace. "I love you, Debbie."

"I know."

They leaped apart as the thud of the knocker echoed through the house.

"Oh, he's here." Abigail dabbed at her face with the wilted handkerchief.

"Calm down," Deborah advised. "Deep breaths. Elizabeth is getting the door."

A moment later, Edward stood in the doorway. He nodded to Deborah with a slight smile, then centered his attention on Abigail.

"Thank you for inviting me," he murmured as he advanced.

Abigail shoved her handkerchief up her sleeve and extended her hand to him.

"It was kind of you to come, Edward. Please, sit down."

She resumed her place on the sofa, and Deborah tiptoed to the window, where she sat down on the cushioned window seat.

She couldn't watch, and she wished she could plug her ears and not hear without being outrageously rude.

Abigail cleared her throat. One quick glance showed Deborah that Edward had sat down beside Abigail on the sofa but was keeping his distance.

He still has hope, Deborah thought. *This will crush him. And how will he feel toward Jacob now? They've been inseparable since boyhood. Will this drive them apart forever?*

She considered her closeness to Abigail. The events of the last week had tested their loyalty, but Deborah knew she would always love her sister. She hoped Edward and Jacob's bond was firm enough to take them through this and bring them out still friends on the other side.

"Edward, I. . ." Abigail cleared her throat.

Deborah stared out the window at the sunlit garden. How she wished she were the little phoebe perched on the syringa bush, chirping in blissful unawareness.

"Edward, I am ready to give you my decision."

Abigail's voice had an icy touch, and Deborah winced. She knew her sister found her task excruciating and had retreated into coldness to make it easier. Tears were no doubt lurking, and she wanted to complete the interview without breaking down.

"I'm ready." Edward's voice was as stony as hers, and Deborah's heart ached for him.

"I. . ."

The pause was too long, and Deborah gritted her teeth, eyes closed. *Tell him! Just tell him.*

After another long moment of silence, Edward's voice came, quiet and gentle now.

"Perhaps I can help you, my dear. You wish to say that you've decided to marry my cousin."

Abigail sighed and whispered, "Yes."

"And you. . .regret any pain you have caused me."

"Very much."

"But you feel this is the only true and honest thing you can do."

"Stop being so. . .so good!"

"How would you have me be?"

Something like a hiccup came from Abigail, and Deborah couldn't resist turning her head ever so slightly and peeking.

Edward was drawing her sister into his arms, but it was not an embrace of passion. Abigail laid her head on his strong shoulder and let her tears flow.

"It will be all right, you know," he said.

"I hope so."

"It will, dear. If God had wanted us together, he wouldn't have kept me away so long."

"Really?"

"Really. I think I saw that when I first came home. I simply didn't want to admit it. But there's no denying it. You love

Jacob, and you were meant to be his wife."

He stroked Abigail's hair and leaned back against the sofa with a sigh.

More than ever, Deborah wished she were not in the room. Yet she was glad in a perverse way that she was allowed to see the true mettle Edward was made of. His heart was breaking, yet he was comforting the one who'd delivered the blow.

She turned back to the window view. The phoebe was gone, but a chipmunk was scurrying about the garden. She felt a tear slide down her cheek and brushed it away with her sleeve.

"So. . .you aren't angry with me?" Abigail asked.

"All is forgiven," he said.

"And Jacob?"

"There's no bitterness between us, nor will there be."

"Thank you, Edward."

The sofa creaked, and their clothing rustled. Deborah turned to see that both had risen.

"Would you please excuse me?" Abigail asked.

"Of course, my dear."

Edward bowed over her hand, then watched her leave the room.

Deborah wondered if he remembered she was there. Should she jump up and offer to fetch his hat? What was the etiquette for ushering out rejected suitors?

He turned slowly, and his thoughtful gaze rested on her in the window seat.

"It seems your duties are ended."

"Oh, yes." She hopped up, her face flushing. "I'm sorry, Edward. It was not my choice to witness that."

"I know." His smile was a bit thin, but even so, it set her pulse tripping. "I believe her declaration was final."

Deborah nodded. "I'm afraid so. She won't change her mind."

They stood for several seconds, looking at each other. At last, Deborah said softly, "My condolences."

"Thank you. Perhaps you'll be kind to me at the wedding, and we'll laugh together about this. That way, maybe folks won't gossip about my despair and desperation."

"Is that what you're feeling now?"

"One thing I learned in my long exile, Deborah, is that God alone controls my destiny."

"So. . .perhaps even this is a part of His providential plan for you?"

"I must say yes to that, decidedly yes, or deny the faith I've gained. It is disheartening now, but I'm sure God can use this disappointment to prepare me for a different future, just as He used the shipwreck to prepare me for this."

Deborah eyed him for a moment, gauging his mood. "Do you have to go back to the office right away?"

"No, I've nothing more exciting than a stack of ledgers to draw me."

"Would you care for lemonade? I'd love to hear more about your experience—if I haven't badgered you enough about it already."

He smiled and nodded. "Lemonade sounds refreshing."

The next hour flew as Deborah plied him with questions about the men who fled the shipwreck with him and about his life on the island. He brought her near weeping again, telling how they had drifted for days in the longboat. Three of the men in the longboat had died and one was lost overboard before they reached the island. He then changed his tone and recounted humorous incidents that he, Gideon, and John went through as they became accustomed to their island home.

"They wouldn't leave off calling me 'sir' at first," Edward said. "Finally I told them, 'Listen, fellows, if we're still here fifty years from now, with our gray beards down to our belts, are you still going to dodder around calling me "sir"?' And Gideon said, 'I'm not sure we'll have belts by then, sir. We may have to eat them if we don't find a way to catch more fish.'"

Deborah shook with laughter, then sobered. "When you were alone after Gideon fell off the cliff, how did you go on? You told me about Kufu, the bird that came to you, but still. . ."

Edward settled back in his chair and sighed. "It was very difficult at first. I thought I would go mad, being alone there. I kept repeating scripture portions to myself and composing imaginary letters to my parents and my sister. And of course, to Abigail."

"That helped you?"

"Yes. I pretended to write long letters, detailing my daily life. Gathering food, improving my shelter against the rainy season, climbing the hills to scout for sail." He shot her a sidelong glance. "I even wrote to you once."

"You did?"

"Yes. I thought it might amuse you. I drew a picture of my hut on a piece of bark, too, then tossed it in the surf, pretending it would float to you, along with my latest letter to. . ."

She smiled. "You must have floated a lot of letters to Abby."

"Hundreds. And later I'd find them washed up on shore down the beach." He sighed and pulled out the pocket watch that had been his father's. "It's getting on toward supper time. I must leave you."

"Won't you—"

He held up one hand to silence her invitation. "I don't think this is the night, but thank you."

She walked with him into the front hall and handed him his hat. It was new, she noted, not his father's old one. His fashion consciousness was probably linked to his hope to win Abigail's hand, but she didn't mind. She only knew that he would hold his own in looks and good manners if dropped in the middle of a group of businessmen and statesmen. And in a roomful of eligible women? Abigail was probably the only woman who wouldn't find him magnetic.

He stood before the door, looking down at her with a half smile on his lips, and she realized she had been staring at him again. Bad habit. She'd have to train herself out of it.

"I wonder, Deborah. . . ."

"Yes?"

His smile spread to his gleaming brown eyes. "I wonder if you and your mother and sister would care to tour Hunter Shipping tomorrow if the weather is fine."

She swallowed a lump that had suddenly cropped up in her throat. Had he not taken Abby seriously? She was sure he had.

"I. . .must discourage you, if you think my sister is not adamant in her choice."

"I'm sure she is. But I mentioned to your mother not long ago that we have some fine fabrics in the warehouse. I thought perhaps you ladies would enjoy coming to the office, and Jacob and I could show you about."

She stared up at him for a moment, amazed at his calmness. He bore his cousin no malice. Could she be as generous to Abby? Her heart fluttered, and she knew that her professed forgiveness of Abigail was genuine. She could give thanks to God for this turn of events. Surely this resolution was part of His greater plan.

eight

It was a bright, sunny day, and the breeze that fluttered in from Casco Bay kept the temperature comfortable. Edward rose early, unable to sleep well, and arrived at the office shortly after seven. He huddled over the ledgers, frowning and trying to find the elusive inconsistency he felt sure was there.

At five minutes to eight, he heard Daniels and the clerks enter the outer office, and a moment later he heard Jacob's brisk step. Edward opened his door, and Jacob came toward him, grinning.

"Still friends, Ed?"

"Of course." Edward grasped his hand. "Congratulations."

"Thank you. I can't tell you what it means to me that you're taking it this way."

Edward smiled. "I shall endeavor not to diminish your joy, cousin. What would you think of inviting all the Bowman ladies down here this afternoon?"

"I like it, but what for?"

He shrugged. "A tour of the place. Another chance to see your fiancée and to let her see you in your place of business. Let them look over the dress goods in the warehouse before we sell them all."

"Splendid idea! Will you make the arrangements?"

"Yes."

Jacob nodded. "Then I'll be in my office." He headed for the far corner of the large room, where two workmen were erecting a wall to enclose a cubicle for his new oak desk. He swung around, still smiling. "I don't suppose this will be finished by the time they get here? And decorated?"

Edward laughed. "Hardly. Would you rather wait until it's done?"

"No, no. Let's invite them today."

By way of an apprentice who swept the floors and sorted bins of hardware, Edward sent a note around to the Bowman house, asking the ladies if they would care to see the improvements at Hunter Shipping, in company with the owner and Mr. Price, and take tea afterward in the office.

The boy came back forty minutes later with a brief but courteous reply. Both the misses Bowman would await him at one o'clock. Their mother was otherwise engaged.

Edward hired a hack after lunch. He and Jacob arrived at the Bowman residence to find the ladies waiting. Abigail was dressed in a burgundy silk walking dress with a feathered hat and white gloves. Deborah's dress was a plain, dark blue cotton, topped with a crocheted shawl and a straw bonnet. Edward was not sure who was prettier—the elegant, refined lady Abigail or the wholesome, restless Deborah. Abigail seemed pleased that they would not have to walk all the way to the docks and back. Although it was a swift twenty-minute stroll for Edward, the commercial district near the harbor was not one that ladies frequented on foot.

"Riding will save you ladies from wearing out your slippers and making the strenuous uphill walk on the way home," Jacob said as he handed Abigail up into the enclosed carriage.

Deborah smiled at that, placing her sturdy leather shoe on the step and hopping up beside her sister, barely putting pressure on Edward's hand for assistance. He could almost read her thoughts: She was not one to glide about in delicate slippers and tire from a brisk walk.

As they rode slowly along the streets, Edward commented on how much the population and commerce of the town had increased during his five years' absence. He was glad he'd worn the new suit he'd had made at his mother's insistence. His hair was neatly trimmed now, too. Still, he could see that Jacob outdid him so far as Abigail was concerned. The greater part of her attention was devoted to his cousin.

When they reached their destination, Edward learned that Abigail had never been onto the wharf. Deborah, it seemed, had ventured there under escort. By whom, Edward did not ask. Abigail shrank from the edge, preferring to be safely flanked by Jacob and Deborah as they walked out past the tinker's shop and the dry goods, hardware, and candle shops to the company's large store. Edward followed a step behind. Sailors and stevedores passed them and stared. The ladies flushed, and Abigail clutched Jacob's arm.

Edward stared down the worst of the oglers and stepped forward to touch Deborah's sleeve.

"Miss Bowman?" He offered his arm. She hesitated only a moment, then laid her hand lightly in the crook of his elbow.

"Thank you," she whispered.

It felt odd having a lady other than his mother on his arm once more, but Edward decided it was pleasant. Deborah's eager anticipation spilled over in her face, and he knew few women he would rather squire about Portland.

As soon as they were inside the store, she pulled away from him, apparently feeling secure on her own now, and wandered about, examining everything. Abigail, however, clung to Jacob's arm and looked about timidly.

Deborah's fascination with the chandlery pleased Edward. She was a practical girl, and her face brightened as she surveyed the mounds of rope and canvas, piles of bolts and pins, and barrels of victuals suitable for ships' crews.

"Your father was a man of great foresight to build his store right on the wharf," she said.

"Actually, my grandfather started the chandlery here with a little shack that offered the most basic supplies. Father improved the establishment, and I have to give my cousin credit for the latest expansion. This entire section is new." He stretched out one arm, indicating the wing Jacob had added to house a wider selection of foods, containers, tools, and hardware.

"Do lots of people come here to buy?" Abigail's voice squeaked. She squeezed nearer to Jacob as a burly seaman pushed past them, nodding and eyeing the ladies.

"Yes," Jacob told her. "The store was begun to outfit Hunter ships and any others that docked at this wharf, but we're open to all customers."

Edward nodded. "That's right. We've built a reputation for offering a wide variety of goods. Of course, we're competing for the business of ships that aren't owned locally. When a vessel comes in from another port—say, Buenos Aires or New York or Amsterdam—we hope it will choose Hunter's Wharf for unloading and selling its cargo."

They left the store and ambled along the wharf toward the city. Abigail seemed more at ease and chatted quietly with Jacob. As they approached the street, Edward pointed up the hill toward the distant observatory tower, built a dozen years previously in Captain Moody's sheep pasture on Munjoy Hill.

"Look! See that flag? There's a ship coming in to dock."

"Is it one of your ships?" Deborah asked.

"I don't know yet. I hope it's the *Prosper.* We'll find out soon enough."

They crossed the busy street that ran along the waterfront, then entered the warehouse.

"This is where we stow outgoing cargo until it's loaded, and incoming until it's sold." Edward guided them out of the way of two men rolling casks down the aisle of crates and barrels. The containers were piled high, and he felt a little claustrophobic when walking between them. He glanced anxiously at Deborah, to see if she was feeling the closeness, but she took in the scene with glittering eyes.

"Well, now. If it isn't my beautiful future daughter-in-law."

They all turned and saw brawny Felix Price approaching with a grin splitting his tanned face. Beads of sweat stood on his brow, and he wiped his hands on his homespun trousers.

"Oh, Mr. Price." Abigail's breathless words were lost in the cavernous warehouse. She ducked her head in acknowledgment of Felix's boisterous greeting.

"I broke the news to my parents last night," Jacob said, his cheeks nearly as red as Abigail's.

"Afternoon, Uncle Felix," Edward said easily, but he kept a sharp watch on the man. Uncle Felix was rough enough that he wouldn't care whether he'd embarrassed his son and his employer or not. That didn't bother Edward, but he was concerned that his uncle had mortified Abigail by calling out such a teasing declaration before the workmen. Several of the laborers paused in their work and cast glances their way but turned back to their tasks when they saw Edward's stern gaze upon then.

"Hello." Abigail's face was by now crimson, but she took the meaty hand extended to her and dipped a curtsey.

Deborah greeted Felix with a charming smile. "Good day, Mr. Price."

"Well, Miss Debbie. What are you doing here? It's not Thursday."

Edward wondered what that meant, but Deborah merely told him, "We're touring Hunter Shipping."

"Well, now, ain't we grand?"

Deborah laughed, but Edward saw Jacob wince as Abigail squeezed his arm. He wondered if her fingernails were digging through Jacob's sleeve into his skin. Felix Price frightened her with his loud, breezy manner, it seemed. Edward wondered what that would bode when Abigail married Jacob.

It was true that his uncle was unpolished. Felix had been known as a ruffian in his youth. He'd fished for years, hauling a living from the ocean by brute force, and was known in those days for drinking quantities of ale when on land and occasionally using his fists in blustery tavern brawls. But Aunt Ruth had fallen in love with him. Though her social status and manner of living were lowered considerably on her wedding day, she still appeared to love him thirty years later and put up with him when his coarseness flared up. Somehow she'd maintained her gentility and was so well liked that Portland's most prestigious women still welcomed her into their parlors.

Felix was another story, and his friends were for the most part fishermen and dockworkers. His employment at Hunter Shipping for the past ten years gave him limited approval. Of course, he was always welcome in the Hunter home, but Felix did not presume on his in-laws' goodness and, for the most part, kept to his own circle. He was good at his job in the warehouse, the men respected him, and he kept the vast quantities of supplies in order.

"We're heading over to the office for tea, Uncle Felix," Edward said.

"Ah, tea for the ladies. I expect you gents have peppermint cakes and gingersnaps with your drinkables." Felix turned to the expanse of the warehouse and shouted, "Come, lads, clear the floor there! We've a ship docking in an hour's time! Look lively!"

They hustled Abigail and Deborah toward the steps leading up to the office, and Edward was thankful to shut the door and the noise behind them.

"You see that little room a-building over there?" Jacob asked Abigail, pointing to the far corner.

"Y—yes."

He smiled down at her. "That, my dear, is my new office. In a week or two when it's finished, I'll bring you down here again to see it."

"It's. . .awfully small, isn't it?"

Jacob laughed. "Well, yes, but it's more than Mr. Daniels, the accountant, has."

"What does he have?"

"A desk over there between the clerks and the record files."

Edward said nothing but caught Deborah's troubled glance. He wished he could reassure her, but he could only smile and lead them into his own office.

In the private room, one of the young clerks laid out tea for four on a small table opposite his desk.

"Abigail, would you mind pouring?" Edward asked.

"Not in the least, thank you."

There. This was going better. While outgoing Deborah might have felt at ease among the workers, Abigail could not hide her relief at escaping into the quiet, well-appointed office. He began to tell them about the nautical artifacts displayed on the walls, and soon she seemed to have regained her composure.

"That's a lovely painting," Abigail said, eyeing the winter landscape.

"Thank you." Edward glanced at his cousin. "I believe that belongs to Jacob and will find its home in his new office when it's finished."

"No need, Ed. Keep it in here if you like it. I only paid a few dollars for it, and it was company money."

Edward smiled. "We'll discuss it later." *After I look up the amount you paid for it,* he told himself. He did not doubt Jacob's word but felt he ought to go slowly in financial matters and verify what the staff told him. If all was as Jacob represented it, he would be glad to let his cousin have the pleasure of hanging the painting on the wall above his desk.

Deborah carried her cup and saucer to the window and peered out.

"You have a splendid view of the wharf and the harbor, Edward."

"Thank you. You've never been here before?"

"Not in the office."

"But you've seen the warehouse."

She smiled at him over her shoulder. "Yes, but Abby hasn't until today."

He smiled and turned to Abigail. "What did you think? We're a rough lot, I'm afraid."

She stirred a spoonful of sugar into her tea and glanced up at him from beneath long lashes. "It's. . .exciting, but I'm afraid I'm not used to such hubbub."

"No, I thought not. I hope our outing didn't unsettle you."

Jacob pulled his chair close to Abigail's. "Edward suggested you and Deborah might want to look over the fabrics we have on hand. I can ask my father to send some boys up here with the bolts if you wish."

"That might be nice," Abigail said, glancing at her sister.

"By all means," said Deborah. "I'm sure Abby will be needing some new dresses soon."

A few minutes later, two of the laborers came in with several bolts of material. They spread them on Edward's desk, and Abigail smiled at them.

"Mr. Price says that's the best of 'em, sir."

"Very good." Edward herded the men out the door.

"Thank you," said Abigail. "I didn't expect this privilege."

Edward shrugged. "You are welcome anytime, Abigail. Jacob can tell you if we get something in that he thinks you would like. When the *Falcon* returns from France, I expect there will be a great number of fancy goods on board."

"Debbie, look at this rose silk."

Deborah set her teacup down and went to join her sister at the desk.

"Edward. . ." Jacob was eyeing him uncertainly.

"Yes?" Edward matched his low tone.

"What do I do if she finds something to her liking?"

He shrugged. "Send it home with her, and send the bill to Dr. Bowman."

Jacob seemed a bit relieved, and Edward wondered, not for the first time, how his return was affecting Jacob's salary. He would have to go over the last few payrolls in detail.

A discreet knock sounded, and he went to the door.

"We've a ship docking, Mr. Hunter," said Daniels.

"We saw the flag before we came in. Is it the *Prosper*?"

Daniels frowned. "No, sir, it's the *Annabel*, out of Philadelphia. She's bringing textiles and wheat, and she hopes to take on lumber. The master's mate came ashore a few minutes ago in a boat. The ship will moor at our dock."

Edward rose. "Shall we take you home, ladies?"

"I'd love to see the ship dock." Deborah's eager brown eyes darted from him to the scene beyond the window.

"I told Mother we'd be home early," Abigail said with a note of reluctance. "Elizabeth was ill this morning, and we need to help with the dinner preparations."

Deborah sighed. "All right. I'd forgotten."

Edward went to the door and told one of the clerks to run out and secure a carriage for them. When he turned back, he saw that Jacob was gathering up the bolt of rose-colored material and smiling at Abigail. Her face bore the most serene expression Edward had seen her wear since his return. Instead of allowing pangs of jealousy or depression to assail him, he sent up a quick prayer of thanks.

"Jacob, perhaps you'd like to see the ladies home," he said. "I'll head for the wharf, and you can meet me there when you return."

"If you're sure you won't need me for half an hour."

"I'm sure."

Edward walked with them out the front door and around to where the hack was waiting. When Jacob and both ladies were aboard, he shut the door.

"I'll be back soon," Jacob said through the window.

"Fine. We'll go over the manifest together." Edward tipped his hat to the sisters and stood back. The driver flicked the reins and headed away from the harbor.

Edward stood still for another moment, trying to analyze his feelings. Why wasn't he upset today? The woman he'd loved for years had jilted him last night. He could only conclude that God had answered his prayers for peace.

As the coach turned out of the yard, Deborah leaned out the window and looked back, waving at him. Her hair had escaped the straw bonnet and flew about her rosy cheeks.

Edward couldn't help smiling. He lifted his hand and waved back.

❧

Late that evening, Edward bent over the ledgers in his father's study at home. No matter how many times he went over the accounts, he could find no fault in Daniels's bookkeeping. Even the price of the painting Jacob had purchased was as he'd represented it. Still, something was amiss. Edward was sure of it. The *Prosper* had brought a good income to the company on every voyage until his father's death. Then she had made a run to the Caribbean that should have been profitable, but instead the goods sold barely covered the expenses for the voyage. Edward totaled the sales three times, then compared his figures to those of the schooner's previous voyages. Perhaps it was poor judgment in the goods purchased in the islands.

The next voyage had brought in a little more but was still far below the amount the *Prosper* usually earned. He then laid the figures side by side with the earnings of the *Falcon* and found that the European trade was far outearning the Caribbean voyages.

Edward ran a hand through his hair and looked at the clock. It was late, and he was tired. Perhaps things would make more sense in the morning.

But the next morning, he saw no more logic to the figures than he had the night before. The custom at Hunter Shipping was for the office staff to work a half day on Saturdays unless a ship was docking. Edward carried the ledgers back to the office and called Mr. Daniels into his private room.

"I see what you mean, Mr. Edward," Daniels admitted after Edward had carefully pointed out the troublesome amounts to him. "I did notice that the last couple of voyages were not so good for the *Prosper*, but I thought it was just one of those things that happens occasionally."

Edward shook his head. "I'm at a loss, Mr. Daniels. But I'm not sure the company ought to consider buying another ship if profits are falling."

"They've increased in other areas."

"Yes. The *Falcon* and the sloop have both done very well on their recent voyages." Edward leaned back in his chair. "I just don't understand it. The Caribbean trade has been our mainstay, and those cargoes were all good products."

"Not as much coffee as we like to get," Daniels mused. "Less of the high-profit items, more of low-profit goods like rice."

"Perhaps you can get me the copies of the *Prosper*'s manifests from these voyages," Edward said. "Now that you say that, I'd like to compare the percentages of different goods she brought back."

"Yes, sir. Perhaps it's just a matter of instructing Captain Stuart on what merchandise you want him to trade for."

Edward flipped the pages of the latest ledger once more. The arithmetic was flawless. Daniels supervised his clerks so closely that Edward was sure they wouldn't make a mistake or change the figures without the accountant noticing it. Daniels was past sixty years of age, and Jeremiah Hunter had treated him well. He earned a good salary and was now a part owner in Hunter Shipping. Edward decided that Daniels had little motive to cheat the company. But wouldn't a man of Captain Stuart's experience know what cargoes to buy? He'd made eight voyages for Hunter Shipping, and up until the last two, he'd seemed to know how to buy goods in high demand at a low price. Was it just a coincidence that the *Prosper* had barely made a profit on its last two voyages south?

nine

Deborah opened the Bowmans' front door a week later and found Edward and Jacob waiting on the doorstep. She had half expected Jacob to come around looking for Abby that evening, but it surprised her to see Edward with him. Of course, they had behaved cordially toward each other the day she and Abby toured the shipping company with them. Now Jacob was laughing at something his cousin had said, and they both turned to face her with smiles on their lips.

For the first time, Deborah saw a family resemblance. Edward was taller by two inches, and his hair and eyes much darker than Jacob's. But the nose was the same, she realized, and both had a somewhat obstinate set to their chins. Jacob's form was more compact, and his legs were shorter, like his father's. But both had broad, muscular shoulders and were clean shaven, though Edward had admitted to her and Abigail that he had worn a beard of necessity for nearly four years. She tried to picture him in a bushy, untrimmed beard, and that set her off in a chortle.

"What's so funny, miss?" Jacob asked, taking a stern posture and stiffening his back.

"Nothing you need to know. Won't you come in?" She forced her mouth into a more serious line as she took their hats. "Unfortunately, Abigail has gone with my mother to call on Mrs. Jordan. But they should be back soon, if you'd care to wait."

"Only if you'll join us," said Edward, and her heart lurched, though she knew he meant nothing special by it.

"What?" Jacob asked in mock horror. "Deborah sitting with us when she doesn't have to? Unheard of."

She showed them to the parlor, then hastened to the kitchen to fix tea. Hurrying back to her guests, Deborah paused in the front hall to glance in the looking glass. Edward had come back, even though Abby had turned him down. Her pulse surged. Did she dare think he enjoyed being here in spite of the blow he had recently received?

Although Edward was still reticent about some aspects of his voyage and sojourn on the island, Jacob was more than willing to talk. He was an excellent storyteller, and Deborah suspected that Abigail had not let him tell as many tales of the sea as he would have liked.

She listened avidly as Jacob recounted the damage sustained by the *Egret*. He coaxed Edward to tell his part of the story, claiming he'd been wondering about certain points.

"How did you find Spring Island? Was it by accident, or did you make for it?"

"It was the captain's choice," Edward said, settling back in his chair with a steaming cup of tea. "He'd brought a compass and a quadrant with him when he climbed down into the boat, as well as a chart and a copy of Bowditch's navigation tables."

"Ah!" Jacob eyes gleamed. "We had a compass, but that was the extent of our navigating tools."

"The winds weren't right for us to head for the Society Islands or the Marquesas," Edward said. "I suggested Hawaii, but Captain Trowbridge said it was more than a thousand miles away. We were much closer to this little island in the middle of nowhere. He wasn't sure we could fetch it, and it would have been disaster if we'd missed it. We all would have died of thirst in another day or two. But through God's grace and the captain's knowledge, we made it."

"It's too bad our boats were separated," Jacob said.

"Yes, but that was part of God's plan, too. I believe that now. He wanted me there with Gideon and John, and at the last of it, by myself for a good long while."

"It's hard for me to fathom why God would want that to happen," Jacob said. "Do you think He wanted the others to die like they did?"

Edward hesitated. "I don't know. He took them home, one by one, and each passing left a deep impression on the rest of us. The two fellows who were with me the longest didn't hold much with prayer and faith at first. John Webber was cocky and proud. He ran wild whenever we touched port. But the captain's testimony before he died influenced John to believe in Christ."

"Praise God," Deborah murmured.

"And when John cut his arm and began to get feverish, Gideon tended him like a baby. During that time, John urged Gideon to turn to the Lord. Afterward, Gideon came to me and told me he'd had a long talk with the Almighty, and he was a child of God from then on. We had precious fellowship together, Gideon and I."

"What a wonderful blessing." Deborah set her china cup down and folded her hands in her lap, ready to hear more.

"Yes. God used the storm and the wreck and all that happened afterward to draw those two men, at least, to Himself."

"I guess I can see that He brought good from it," Jacob said. "I'm glad they believed. It's still hard for me to thank God for letting the ship sink, though."

Deborah smiled at Edward, and he answered her, his eyes full of understanding. Their gazes locked for a long moment, and she felt warmth flooding through her chest and up to her face as the blood went to her cheeks.

Edward was such a dear brother in Christ. If only God would bring a man like him to love her the way Edward had loved Abby. She would not, could not, allow the thought to reach beyond that. On other occasions, she'd felt the flutter of longing in her heart when she and Edward conversed. They comprehended each other perfectly. Hadn't Abby felt that when she talked to him? How could she not yearn to be with him?

Even these thoughts made her feel uneasy, as she vaguely discerned an uncrossable line. Edward loved Abby. She could wish for a man like him, and she could wish for his future happiness, but she could not meld those two wishes into one. It would be scandalous.

She broke the stare with regret and caught Jacob's eye. He was settling against the back of his chair with a contented smile that she hoped wasn't a smirk.

Oh no! He's imagining things between Edward and me. Or was it her imagination? The sudden prospect that she had betrayed her sister by developing strong feelings for Edward slammed Deborah's heart. She was fooling herself if she refuted it.

What had Jacob seen, exactly? Worse yet, what did he think he had seen? She could not deny the undercurrent that had surged between her and Edward. But it wouldn't be proper to act upon it. Would it? Abby had definitely put an end to Edward's hopes and was planning her wedding to Jacob. It was wrong for Deborah to feel an attraction for her sister's rejected suitor. Of course, Edward didn't feel anything of the sort for her. Did he? And if he did, he was too much of a gentleman to do anything about it so soon. But Jacob's perception of what occurred was another matter entirely.

"Edward is considering sailing down to Portsmouth in our sloop soon to look at a ship for sale there," Jacob said.

Edward's features sobered. "Yes, we're thinking of adding one more vessel to our fleet. I'm looking over the accounts to be sure we're in good enough financial shape for that."

"I thought it was settled," Jacob said, turning toward him with his eyebrows arched. "You said you would go and size up the ship we spoke of."

Deborah saw Edward's troubled frown, but she decided this topic was a good distraction for Jacob. It was much better than the flutter of guilt she'd felt a moment ago. "When are you going?" she asked Edward.

"I'm not sure."

Jacob said, "We're waiting on our schooner the *Prosper*."

"We don't want to lay out any large sums of money until she brings in her cargo," Edward explained. "But Jacob expected her back several weeks ago. We've been watching for her since I returned."

"Where did she sail?" Deborah picked up the teapot, and Jacob held out his cup for her to refill.

"To the Caribbean," he said. "Captain Frost of the *Eden* brought me a packet of letters two months past. Said he'd met the *Prosper* a hundred miles north of Havana and exchanged mail with her. The report I received from our captain indicates the *Prosper* was doing fine at that time, but we've heard nothing since."

"Perhaps she's waiting on her return cargo," Deborah said.

Jacob winced and shook his head. "I wish I knew. If she's been pirated or sunk—"

"Let's not borrow trouble." Edward threw Deborah a reassuring smile.

"How many men aboard?" she asked.

"Twenty-four," said Edward.

Jacob sighed. "Both the Ramsey brothers are part of the crew, and Ivory Mason's son. Lots of local boys. The company can't afford to lose another ship, but beyond that, the loss of the crew would devastate this town."

"Then we must pray for the best," Deborah said.

"Yes." Edward gave his cousin a slight nod, as though he'd reached a decision. "As soon as she docks and the cargo is unloaded, I will run down to Portsmouth and look at the *Resolute*." He swiveled toward the hall, and Deborah heard the sound of the front door opening.

She jumped up. "That must be Mother and Abby."

Mrs. Bowman and Abigail joined them in the parlor, and Deborah hurried to the kitchen to get a fresh pot of tea and more cups. When she returned to the front room, all four were engaged in lively conversation about the choosing of Portland as the new state of Maine's capital and the preparations underway to celebrate statehood.

Deborah poured tea for Mother and Abigail and sat on a Windsor chair tucked near the hearth and watched them all. Edward and Jacob did not seem to compete for Abigail's favor. Both participated in the discussion equally, with courteous but opinionated contributions.

Edward turned to Deborah after a few minutes. "What do you think, Debbie? Should the people be taxed to build new government buildings?"

"Well, why not? We begged for statehood. We must bear the consequences."

She wondered if he was just being polite, including her in the conversation. But his smile made her feel that it was more than that. Edward cared what she thought. The idea that a man she esteemed found her thoughts worth considering brought on a surge of pleasure that was followed by a confusing blast of self-recrimination. She could not, must not consider Edward as anyone more than a friend at this time. It would shock society if he took up with the sister of the girl who had so recently rejected him. But the very idea made Deborah's chest tighten. If Edward *should* think of her in that way—it was too intoxicating to contemplate.

Edward turned his attention to her mother as she inquired about his family, and Deborah shrank into her corner and watched the others. Jacob was fully engrossed in Abigail. He even chatted with her for several minutes about the style of gown she was sewing for the new governor's upcoming ball.

Deborah searched Edward's profile for signs of jealousy but found none. He conversed with Deborah and her mother while Jacob and Abigail continued their chat in low tones, with eyes for no one else in the room. Deborah drew in a long, slow breath. Edward had not come here to pine for Abby or to torture himself by watching his cousin court the one he loved. And she doubted he found her mother's prattle about the neighbors overly absorbing.

She peeked at him. His attention to her mother's small talk was flawless, yet. . . He threw a quick smile her way, and Deborah's lungs suddenly felt too small to hold the same air he breathed.

❧

Ten days later, Edward put on his hat and headed for the front door of his family home. He stopped with his hand on the marble knob.

"I hate to go off to the office and leave you alone, Mother. With Jenny sick—"

"What claptrap! Do you suppose I've never been alone before?"

"Well, no, but. . ." He looked her over and saw a capable, healthy woman with graying hair, a figure leaning toward stoutness, glinting brown eyes, and a determined scowl.

"Besides, I shan't be alone. You'll come home for dinner, and I shall have company for tea at half past three."

"Oh." Edward was taken aback by his gentle mother's spirited declaration. He supposed she had grown more independent of necessity since his father's death.

"Yes, and good company, too."

She seemed to be dangling that morsel in front of him, teasing him to jump at it, so he said rather cautiously, "Anyone I'm acquainted with?"

"Deborah Bowman comes to tea once a fortnight. She's more entertaining than a gossip, and more sympathetic than a parson. Today is Debbie's Tuesday, and there's no one I'd rather share a pot of tea with."

Edward smiled, wondering how this bit of information had managed to elude him. "You make me wish I were invited."

"Well, you're not."

He left the house, still savoring his mother's roguish behavior. She was back to her old self. Or perhaps not. This was a new self. She'd gained a verve that assured him she would be all right now, no matter what God placed in her path.

Her delight at the prospect of tea with Deborah was comforting, too. It told him she'd been enjoying the young woman's company for some time. Since his father's death, perhaps. Deborah was a good listener with an unfailingly cheerful outlook. Only once or twice had he seen her frown over Abigail's standoffish behavior toward him, tiny wrinkles in her smooth disposition. In fact, during the three weeks since Abigail had freed him of his need to look only at her, he'd been taking some rather long looks at Deborah and had decided that her character was altogether pleasing. She matched him in intellect and energy. The idea that Deborah had been bringing sunshine and friendship to his widowed mother brought a warm feeling to his heart.

It also reminded him of his duty to the families of the men of the *Egret*. He'd been to visit the captain's widow a couple of days after he arrived home. Several days later he called on Amos Mitchell's family, and yesterday morning he'd been to see Gideon Bramwell's parents. Those visits were difficult, but the appreciation showered on him told him those interviews had been essential. The parents and wives of the sailors wanted to know how their men had fared to the end.

Gideon Bramwell's mother wept openly when Edward told her about the young man's valiant struggles for survival and their camaraderie on the island. His father shed tears as well when Edward got to the recounting of Gideon's death. He didn't suffer, Edward assured them. His fall from the cliff was unexpected and swift. He died at once on the rocks, and his last act was one of trying to provide food for himself and Edward.

He would try to get to the Wilkes farm tomorrow. It was several miles out of town, but he could borrow a horse and ride out there. Davy's death must have been a severe blow to his parents and the other children. Edward had already discussed with Jacob and Mr. Daniels giving a sum of money to the families of the men who had died when the *Egret* foundered. He himself wanted to take to the Wilkeses the amount allotted to them and tell them how bravely the boy had met his end. It wouldn't be easy, and he wasn't sure how much to tell them about Davy's suffering after he shattered his leg while escaping the *Egret*. Best wait and see what their mood was, he decided. It had been four years, but they might still be angry or bitter toward the company. If the mother seemed resentful or distraught, he would keep to himself the details of the boy's infection and lingering death.

He sighed, knowing he must take a day from his arduous work at the office to accomplish that errand. For the past week he'd given all the time he could spare to his scrutiny of the company's records. It relieved him in some measure, as he'd concluded that Daniels was trustworthy beyond a doubt.

But his study had also given him cause for further dismay. Something was definitely odd about the *Prosper*'s recent record. The ship had been a gold mine for the past two or three years, but since his father's death, she had been marginally profitable. Since Jacob had taken the company's helm, something had gone amiss in the Caribbean trade. Edward didn't like to think his cousin was directly responsible, but he had to eliminate the possibility. He weighed the option of a frank confrontation with Jacob against waiting for the *Prosper* to come in and assessing her performance on the most recent voyage. The longer the ship was delayed, the darker his thoughts were running.

"Edward! Good morning!"

He looked up to see Pastor Jordan approaching him.

"May I walk with you?"

"Certainly. I'm only going to my office."

"I'm heading for a house down past the wharves," the pastor said. "An old salt who lives down there is ill, perhaps dying. Micah Carson."

"I know him," Edward said. "He worked for my father at one time."

"And how are things going with you?"

Edward gritted his teeth. "Well, you made the announcement in church on Sunday, so you know Miss Bowman has set her heart on another."

The pastor nodded, his features schooled to neutrality. "Yes. I wasn't surprised when Dr. Bowman came to see me and asked me to announce Abigail's upcoming marriage to Mr. Price, but I was concerned about you. How are you holding up?"

Edward sighed and looked at the kindly pastor. "The first time I saw her, several weeks ago, I thought I couldn't go on living if she wouldn't have me."

"And now?"

He shrugged, looking down the street toward the harbor. "Well, I'm still alive."

The pastor laid a hand on Edward's shoulder for a moment. "It's a difficult situation, son. I've been praying for you."

"Thank you. I believe the Lord has brought about what is best. I bear Jacob no malice."

"That's good. Look to God for guidance and keep a forgiving spirit."

"I believe I'm more than halfway there."

"Good. This is a time of transition, then, in your mind and in your heart."

"Yes. We are all sifting the meal, so to speak, trying to get the lumps out. Jacob and I had a long talk when I first got home. I've accepted this as God's will for all of us. Now I'm concentrating on the business."

"A big responsibility with your father gone."

"Yes. I'm going over all the records to make sure I know everything that's happened at Hunter Shipping since I went away. I'm afraid our accountant, Mr. Daniels, finds me a bit tedious with all the questions I've been asking him this last month."

"Ah, well, hard work can be a blessing in times of emotional turmoil."

"Would you keep praying for me, Pastor? There are a couple of matters giving me some anxiety."

"Oh? Anything I can help with?"

Edward thought for a moment about the discrepancy in the Caribbean trade. That was strictly a business affair. But the other—an image of Deborah listening avidly as he related his adventures—flitted through his mind. Her smile was so genuine, so yearning that he couldn't help being drawn to her. Just thinking of her these days caused his pulse to jump. Yes, the second one was a matter of the heart.

"Not specifically," he said, "but knowing you are praying for me will be an encouragement."

"Then rest easy," said the pastor. "I've been praying for your peace and a bright future for you ever since I learned you'd come home."

They had neared the harbor, and Edward looked out over the calm water of the estuary. The morning mist was disappearing off the sea. He drew a deep draft of the salty air. His problems with Abigail had dissipated much like the fog, and a new anticipation gripped him. What would God reveal for him, now that the future he'd expected was gone?

ten

Deborah climbed the attic stairs in the Hunter house, preceding her hostess to the door at the top. It opened onto the roof, where a small platform was enclosed by a decorative white railing. She looked out over the town, which in recent years had burgeoned into a city. The cupola on top of the new courthouse caught her eye. So many buildings that hadn't been there when Edward went away. And now the new statehouse was under construction next to the courthouse. Portland must seem huge to him.

When he'd left, the businesses were still reeling from the economic blow dealt by the recent war with England. But now Exchange Street bustled with new shops, the wharves were crowded with stores, and dozens of brigs and schooners filled the harbor. The fledgling legislature was putting the new state constitution in place. Manufacturing was booming—foundries, ropewalks, soap and candle works, and mills and builders. Everywhere one looked, an air of prosperity hung over Portland.

Mrs. Hunter came behind her, puffing up the last few stairs, and stepped up onto the "widow's walk" with Deborah.

"You have such a lovely view of the city and the harbor." Deborah turned to the west and leaned on the railing, letting the wind blow against her face, tugging and teasing at her hair and her straw bonnet. "You must be able to see almost as far as Captain Moody can."

"Oh no, the observatory is much higher than we are." Mrs. Hunter chuckled. "Have you ever been up there?"

"No."

"My husband took me up soon after it was built. We

100

could see the White Mountains of New Hampshire. The captain said he can spot ships forty miles out to sea with his telescope."

Deborah turned and looked east toward the conical building that towered over Moody's homestead. Built on a rise that was one of the high points of the area, it rose majestically over the town, like a lighthouse that had given up the sea, wandered inland, and settled on a farm.

"It is a lot higher," she conceded, "but I like your house best. I can see all the church steeples, the courthouse, and the river and the back cove. Even the cemetery. But I'm right here in your peaceful house."

"Thank you, dear. It's been a snug home for many years. My husband's father saw that it was well built, and I've not had much trouble with it, though I expect Edward will need to have it reshingled before too many more years pass. You can see down there on the gable where the shingles look a bit ruffled."

Deborah squinted down at the edge of the roof. "Yes, I see the spot."

"If we get another bad storm with a high wind from the east, he may need to do it sooner," Mrs. Hunter said with a resigned smile. "But that's the way it is when you live near the sea. Wind, wind, wind."

Indeed, the gusts were pulling at Deborah's bonnet so sharply that she untied the wide strings that anchored it under her chin and took it off, holding it down against her skirt.

"Now you'll lose your hairpins." Mrs. Hunter raised her voice against the stiff breeze, but she was smiling.

"That's a lovely idea." Deborah reached up and probed her coiled hair, extracting several polished wooden pins and slipping them into her pocket. Her long brown locks tumbled about her shoulders and swirled around her face, tossed about by the restless air from the bay.

Mrs. Hunter laughed. "Ah, to be young again."

"Are you cold?" Deborah asked, noting that the older woman pulled her shawl tighter about her.

"Perhaps a bit."

"Then we must go down. I'm sure our tea is ready." Deborah took her hostess's arm and guided her back to the entrance.

Passing through the attic, Deborah noticed chests and disused furnishings crowding the room.

"The castoffs of many generations," Mrs. Hunter said with a smile. "I suppose I ought to go through it all and dispose of half of it, but it seems such a lot of trouble. I believe I'll let Edward do it one day."

Deborah smiled and ran her hand over a smooth old wooden frame. "Did you ever use this loom?"

"No, not me. That belonged to my late husband's grand-mother. Lucy Hamblin Hunter, she was. They say she wove the finest linen in the province. Of course, there weren't too many weavers in Maine then to compete with her."

Deborah laughed. "I admire her patience. It's all I can do to crochet a doily."

"Sometime I will show you the table linen she wove. I have several pieces she made. Why, it must have been almost a hundred years ago now. They say she married her husband while he was in prison."

Deborah stared at her in the dim light, wondering if Mrs. Hunter was teasing her. "In prison? What for?"

"Murder. Nothing less. But he was acquitted, and he and Lucy lived a long and happy life together in a little cabin not many miles from here. It was their son who went to sea and became the first Captain Hunter."

"I like that story." Deborah took Mrs. Hunter's hand and walked slowly down the steps with her. When they had descended into the upstairs hall and the attic door was shut behind them, she said, "Thank you for taking me up. I do love it on the widow's walk."

Mrs. Hunter smiled and patted her arm. "It's a joy to me

when I see your face light up. I don't go up so much myself. . . not since Jeremiah died, God rest his soul."

"You do miss him a lot, don't you?" Deborah walked slowly with her toward the main staircase.

"Every minute I miss him. I used to go up there and look over at the docks. I can see the warehouse from up there. Sometimes I would see him turning the corner of the street on his way home. I'd wave to him, then rush down the stairs to meet him." Her dreamy smile told Deborah she was off in another, more pleasant time. "But then, with him and Edward both dead, as we all supposed, I stopped going up to the roof. It seemed too morbid. I didn't want folks saying, 'There's the widow mourning her menfolk' and pitying me."

"People don't pity you," Deborah assured her. "You're far too alive. You don't mope about."

"Don't I?"

Mrs. Hunter's eyes twinkled, and Deborah laughed.

"No, you most decidedly don't."

"Well, in any event, climbing those stairs is getting to be quite an exertion for me."

"Come," Deborah said. "I smell something tasty."

A few minutes later, they were seated in Mrs. Hunter's cozy sitting room. Deborah much preferred it to the larger front parlor. This small, paneled room was full of bright cushions and enameled boxes of many colors and designs. She knew that Mr. Hunter had presented the boxes to his wife one at a time, either when he returned from a voyage or when a ship docked after a long trading excursion, laden with exotic wares. When Deborah visited, her hostess let her handle and admire them as much as she liked. She fingered the brightly painted ones from the Orient as the maid laid out their refreshment.

After Jenny had left the room, Deborah sat down and Mrs. Hunter poured out their tea.

"Quite an announcement after church on Sunday."

"Yes." Deborah busied herself with the sugar tongs, not

sure she could meet the lady's gaze without bursting out in either laughter or tears. The public reading of the marriage intentions of Mr. Jacob Price and Miss Abigail Bowman had left her torn.

"You don't seem elated at the news. But then, neither do you seem dismayed."

Deborah couldn't help smiling then. "You must understand my mixed feelings. I'm happy for my sister, but only because she is happy."

"Tut! My nephew Jacob is a good lad. He's risen above his father's humble station. He has his mother's wits."

"It wasn't my intent to disparage Jacob," Deborah said. "I believe he will make Abby a good husband."

"But?"

"But I feel disappointed for Edward."

Mrs. Hunter snorted and set her teacup down. "Edward is not weeping. Neither should you be."

Deborah blinked. It was an alien concept that Edward might be pleased with Abby's rejection of him. Was he relieved to be freed from their engagement? She wondered what he had told his mother after Abby revealed her decision to him. Was it possible that in time he might think of courting another? Of course, that would be the natural course of things after his wounded heart had healed, but how feasible was it that he would be captivated by a woman he considered an adolescent tomboy? Deborah shoved the thoughts away. She didn't dare hope that he might turn his affections her way. He was a family friend now. That was all. It meant nothing, and she mustn't read too much into the recent visit he'd made with Jacob.

She reached for a raisin cake and smiled at her hostess. "All right. I shall cease mourning the rift between him and Abby."

"As is proper. This is a time to rejoice with your sister."

Deborah bit into the cake, considering that. For the past few days, she'd felt more like rejoicing than she had since the day she first saw Edward returned from the deeps. But she was afraid to let her heart run too far astray. Every time she thought much about Edward and her growing feelings for him, she felt guilty. And when she considered whether or not he might ever return them, she felt obliged to quickly stifle that train of thought. She would only lay herself open for disappointment if he did not reciprocate. Time to change the subject.

"Mm, this cake is delicious. Did you make it, or did Jenny?"

"She did," Mrs. Hunter said. "I'm lucky to have that girl. She has a proper touch with the bake oven. But neither she nor I can wait to try cooking on the new stove my son has ordered for me."

"You are getting a cookstove?"

"Yes, I am. It will be prodigious fun. Would you like to come round when it's here and practice with me?"

"I'd love to."

Mrs. Hunter nodded. "We can make a huge pot of chicken stew without stooping over a hearth or catching sparks on our skirts. We'll do it on a Thursday, and you and Abigail can take it around to the widows and orphans."

"That would be wonderful. Some of them are so poor they rarely have meat on their tables."

"Then we'll do it and bake a basket full of biscuits from white flour to go with it."

"That will be a scrumptious treat for them. Does this mean you will share with me your secret for making biscuits?"

Mrs. Hunter paused as if it were a novel thought, then smiled. "I believe I shall. But you must be careful whom you share it with."

"I shall indeed."

They shared a smile of conspiratorial friendship.

"Of course," Mrs. Hunter said primly, "if Edward had married your sister, I'd have told her."

The implications of this were not lost on Deborah, and she

felt her face flush.

"Abby didn't mean to be unkind to him."

"Of course not. But my Edward was always adventurous, perhaps more than she realized. And I'll not deny his experience of the last five years has changed him. He's more passionate now, more eager to make his mark on the world. I suppose that's because he nearly lost the chance."

Deborah tilted her head to one side, mulling that over. Everyone had agreed that Jacob had done fine while he was in charge of the business, and Mrs. Hunter had no complaints about his management. But Edward would do better than fine. His plans for the company, which he'd discussed with her father after the service on Sunday, were ambitious and bold. He would put his heart into the business and run with it, making Hunter Shipping even greater if God would allow it.

"Perhaps you are right," she said to his mother. "His new passion is an extension of his fight for survival on the island."

"You see that, don't you? But your sister feels safer and more at home with Jacob's more placid nature." Mrs. Hunter nodded and raised her cup to her lips. "I expect they'll make a good match."

"I do hope so. I was a bit put out with her when she turned Edward down."

"No need of that. This is well and good."

"You believe that?"

"With all my heart." As the lady reached for a cookie, Jenny Hapworth hurried into the room, her eyes downcast.

"I'm sorry, ma'am, but one of the clerks just came up from the office with a note for you."

She held a slip of parchment out to Mrs. Hunter. Deborah used the interruption to pour more tea into her thin china cup.

"It's a ship." Mrs. Hunter's merry brown eyes filled with anticipation. "Edward sent this to tell me."

"One of their own ships?"

"He's not certain yet."

"Let's pray that it is the *Prosper*." Deborah set the teapot down with care.

"Yes, indeed."

Mrs. Hunter reached out to her, and they clasped hands.

"Father on high, smile upon us today and bring the wayward vessel the *Prosper* safely to port."

Deborah added her own quiet plea. "Dear Lord, please allow us to rejoice in the homecoming of the *Prosper* today. And if this is not that ship, then, Father, we beg you to keep all the men aboard her safe, wherever they be now, and draw her swiftly back to these shores."

They raised their heads and smiled hopefully at one another.

"Why don't you run up to the widow's walk?" Mrs. Hunter suggested. "I'm not up to making the climb again so soon, but you can go and watch."

"How will I know if it's the *Prosper*? She's probably still far down the bay."

"Here." Mrs. Hunter rose and took a small brass spyglass from the cherry sideboard. "You'll be able to see her when she rounds the point and enters the river, but before that, Captain Moody will know. He's already raised the flag for Hunter Shipping, letting the merchants know, so he's identified the vessel. Either he knows her by her lines, or she's hoisted a signal for him."

"That seems promising, doesn't it?"

"Yes, it does. Run along up, dear."

Deborah seized the spyglass and dashed up the two flights of stairs. The wind was worse than ever, and she hadn't bothered to put her hat or her shawl on. Her skirt billowed behind her as she faced east, and her hair whipped about, stinging her cheeks.

She turned to the sea first and tried to see what Moody had seen, but the headland opposite the town, across the Fore River, obstructed her view. So she trained the glass on Moody's observatory. Three banners were flying, but she picked out the one for Hunter's easily. Everyone in town knew the flags of the big shipping companies.

A sudden fear that it was not the long-awaited ship came over her, and she closed her eyes, sending up a frantic petition.

Father, please don't let them lose another ship. There's been enough grief and loss. Please!

Far in the distance, the prow of a ship rounded the cape and entered the river. She held the spyglass to her eye. The national flag flew from the mainmast—and below it the banner of Hunter Shipping!

She turned and ran down the stairs. Jenny and Mrs. Hunter stood in the front hall, where the stairs came down, and a thin boy was with them. Deborah's heart lurched with joy as she heard his pronouncement.

"She's the *Prosper*, all right! Mr. Edward's dancing a hornpipe on the wharf, ma'am."

eleven

Edward carried a sack of sugar up the companionway to the deck of the *Prosper* and heaved it onto the stack near the gangplank. He went back to the hatch and watched two stevedores climb up and deposit their burdens on the pile.

That was it. The ship's cargo was unloaded. All of the previous day and most of this morning, his men had labored at stripping the hold. Under Uncle Felix's exacting command, they'd filled the warehouse and stacked hundreds of barrels and crates in the warehouse yard and along the wharf.

Now the merchants of Portland would swarm to the yard and the wharf to look over the goods and speak for those they wished to purchase.

Edward retrieved his jacket from where he'd hung it on a peg over one of the scuppers but didn't put it on. He was sweating and filthy from his effort. He knew Jacob was on the wharf checking off the manifest that listed the cargo. And Jacob was, without doubt, cool and neat, impeccably attired for a businessman.

That was all right, but Edward preferred to get in among the men and put his back into it. That gave him a better understanding of the men's work and boosted the laborers' opinion of him. It also made the ridiculously generous check Mr. Daniels had written him last week for his monthly salary more acceptable.

Had his father drawn that much from the company every month? His mother assured him that his father had when things were going well. In tight times, such as during the war with England or in the months following the loss of the *Egret* and her cargo, he took less. He always made sure the employees were paid first, from the dockhands to the ship captains. The clerks, the sailors, and the boy who swept the warehouse floor were paid before Mr. Hunter drew his check. That knowledge gave Edward a new appreciation for his responsibility as head of the firm. Scores of families depended on him and Hunter Shipping.

More than ever, he knew he must uncover the mystery of the *Prosper*'s lagging profits. He'd handled the cargo himself and watched every cask and bundle brought up from the hold. If all was not as it should be, now was the time to discover it.

He slung his jacket over one shoulder and headed down the gangplank. The men worked about him in an orderly swarm, toting the sacks, rolling the casks, piling crates on small carts, and pulling the carts along the wharf toward the warehouse.

Jacob called to him as he approached his post near the store.

"Well, Mr. Hunter, you've been exercising your muscles, I see!"

Edward flipped the dripping hair out of his eyes. "To the point of soreness. I've only been back in the office four weeks, and already I'm getting soft."

"Well, I can put you in the warehouse under my father if you wish. That used to be your position, did it not?"

"Yes, before I went to sea as a cabin boy at fourteen."

Jacob nodded with a wry smile. "I had much the same experience, as you know, and I can tell you I prefer the deck to the warehouse floor. Of course, the office is better than either."

Edward laughed. "It wouldn't hurt you to rub shoulders with your old cronies now and then."

"Probably not, but I have a dinner engagement later. I can't see a lady receiving a gentleman in your condition." Jacob's nose wrinkled as he eyed Edward's sweat-drenched shirt.

"That bad?" Edward pulled his chin in and looked down at his clothing. "You're right. Perhaps I'd better go home to wash up and change my clothes."

"Commendable idea," Jacob murmured. "I've put the word out that we'll be open to buyers at noon. Several well-placed merchants will wish to greet you this afternoon as they do their business, I'm sure."

Edward nodded and glanced about to make sure none of the workmen were near enough to overhear. "There's something we need to discuss later, Jacob."

His cousin's eyebrows shot upward. "Anything serious?"

"Perhaps."

Jacob nodded. "At the close of business, then."

Edward bypassed the office and went straight home. He'd have to start taking an extra shirt to work with him to have on hand for such occasions. One of the clerks could fetch him wash water; they heated tea water on a small stove. Yes, he would implement the plan at once. That way he could take all the exercise he wanted and not embarrass Jacob or Mr. Daniels when the upper-class customers came around.

Was this the day his mother had said Deborah would visit? No, that was Tuesday. Time blurred with the hectic unloading of the ship, but he was sure this wasn't the day. Still, he half hoped he would run into Deborah at the house. Looking down once more at his soiled clothing and realizing how filthy he was, he cringed. No, it would not be the best time to meet the woman he hoped most to impress.

The thought startled him, but at once the sharpness of it softened. Why hadn't he seen earlier what a wonderful person Deborah was? Not that she needed impressing. She would scoff at that idea. She didn't judge people by appearances. That first afternoon, when he'd gone to the Bowman house fresh off the ship, she'd welcomed him joyfully, bedraggled as he was.

The image of Deborah's subdued beauty leaped to his mind, her lovely brown eyes and gleaming mahogany hair. She didn't play up her attributes, and many people probably would say she was not as pretty as her sister. Edward had thought so, too, at one time. Now he was beginning to revise that opinion.

His mother thought she was beautiful, and she was a good judge of such things. "Deborah has looks that will last," she'd said just the other day. He hadn't told his mother about his newly kindled feelings for the younger Miss Bowman, but somehow, she seemed to know. Deborah's name came into the dinner conversation almost every evening at the Hunter house.

Yes, she was lovely. On Sunday, she had sat between Abigail and her mother in the family pew. Jacob sat with the family on Abigail's other side, but Edward didn't mind. He took his place beside his mother, but he had eyes only for Deborah, two rows ahead of them that morning. Her green gown was plainer than Abigail's flounced and frilled blue, but it enhanced her creamy skin and dark eyes. And he noticed that while Abby fidgeted during the sermon and cast veiled glances at Jacob throughout the hour, Deborah sat still and seemed to give her undivided attention to Pastor Jordan.

Traits he used to find amusing in Abigail—her flickering attention, her interest in fashion—he had attributed to her immaturity in the old days. But she was a grown woman now, and she had not changed. Deborah, on the other hand, seemed to have grown into a mixture of practicality and playfulness. She appeared to be unconcerned about her appearance beyond neatness and appropriate attire. He knew her to be loyal—look at the way she'd insisted Abby not slough him off. She was industrious, too; she often brought needlework with her to the parlor while entertaining guests when she could have sat idle, and on several occasions, he'd seen her jump to aid her mother with some household task. If his mother's words were any indication, she was a reliable and sensible young woman.

As he approached his home, he tried to squelch all thoughts

of Deborah. They still felt wrong somehow. For more than five years he'd dreamed of a future with Abigail. But the Abigail of his daydreams didn't match up with the Abigail he knew now. Was it possible that the Abigail he'd longed for during his years of exile was more like the actual Deborah?

In confusion, he bounded up the steps and into the house to greet his mother and explain why he had come home. He was grateful it was not Tuesday, after all. He wouldn't have the slightest idea what to say to Deborah.

⋅⋅⋅

An hour later, Edward was back at the warehouse, watching the commotion from the top of a loading platform as buyers thronged the premises, touching the fabrics, sampling the molasses, and sniffing the fruit. Market days at the warehouse were a jumble of colors and scents. When a ship docked, word spread in a flash through the town, and the buyers awaited word that the unloading was completed and the newly arrived wares were available for sale. The merchants hurried in to speak for quantities of goods for their stores, but individuals were just as ardently in search of a bargain at a low price.

His uncle came to stand beside Edward.

"There's your fortune, boy. Your ship came in at last, and all your financial obligations are met and then some."

"Yes," Edward agreed. "God be praised. She was delayed for loading and revictualing, and then she ran into muddy weather in the Caribbean and had to replace torn canvas."

Felix nodded. "Two days ago, we feared she was lost—but she's here now, and all is well."

Edward nodded. He'd read Captain Stuart's report of the voyage, but even with the foul weather and other obstacles accounted for, the *Prosper* had made poor time. She'd brought back a full cargo, which seemed to make everyone else happy; however, the month lost on what should have been a quick run had cost the firm plenty, and Edward was not entirely satisfied with the list of products she'd delivered. He had already asked to have the ship's log on his desk by close of business today.

"Mr. Hunter!"

He turned toward Jacob's voice. His cousin always addressed him formally when employees or customers were listening. Jacob was below him on the floor of the warehouse, holding a long sheet of parchment and beckoning for him to join him and the two men with him.

Edward nodded to Uncle Felix and headed for the steep steps. Just as he was about to descend, he glanced out over the warehouse and halted.

A woman in a brown and blue plaid dress was making her way through the barrels of food and piles of bulging sacks near the door. It couldn't be—

She turned, and the sunlight streaming through the open door glinted on her rich, reddish-brown hair. A young man was with her, a gangly, teenaged boy he didn't recognize, carrying a large basket. As he watched, Deborah began taking yams from a barrel and loading them into the basket.

"Edward? Are you coming down?"

Jacob had come to stand just beneath him, not quite masking his impatience. Edward hastened down the steps.

"I just saw Deborah."

Jacob swiveled around to look but seemed unconcerned.

"What's she doing here?"

"She often comes when we hold open market." Jacob turned and pushed people aside to reach the two men he'd been dealing with, and Edward followed, losing track of Deborah. Ladies didn't venture into a crush like this where bankers and dockhands mingled.

"You know Mr. Engle," Jacob said.

"Yes, hello." Edward shook hands with the gray-haired owner of a sawmill on the edge of the river.

"This is his supervisor, Mr. Park, who is in charge of the lumbering operation. They are interested in sending a load of lumber and barrel staves to St. Thomas."

Edward nodded. "The *Prosper* will put out for the Caribbean and Rio again in two weeks."

"Yes," Jacob said. "If you can have it on the wharf next week, we'll make room for it."

"What about your bigger ship?" Engle asked.

Jacob ducked his head in acknowledgment. "The *Falcon* will be in soon, but she plies the European trade for us. We've new cargo lined up for Amsterdam, LeHavre, Bordeaux, and Lisbon."

"Ah, then the *Prosper* it is. We've a large order. I hope you can take it all at once."

"Mr. Engle has shipped lumber with us before," Jacob said, and Edward nodded.

"Well, then, perhaps you could take these gentlemen into the office and arrange the transaction," he suggested, looking toward the front of the huge room, hoping to spot Deborah again.

"We hope to add a third schooner to our fleet soon," Jacob said to Engle and Park. "If that purchase works out, we'll add the *Resolute* to our West Indies trade."

"You boys are doing well," Park said. "When will you have the new ship?"

"If we decide to buy her, we should have her here inside a week," Jacob replied. "Mr. Hunter leaves tomorrow for Portsmouth to examine the vessel."

"Yes, but we're not certain yet we want to buy her," Edward said, scanning the crowd. "If we do, it will likely take us several weeks to refit her before she's ready to take on cargo."

His mind was only half on the conversation, and then only because he was afraid Jacob would promise cargo space where there was none as yet. He spotted the plaid material of Deborah's dress as the people close to her separated and surged around her.

"Could you gentlemen excuse me, please? There's someone

I must have a word with."

He made his way as quickly as he could through the throng, but when he got to the crates of tea where he'd last seen her, she was gone. He gawked about, feeling foolish, but soon located her and the boy a few yards away.

"Deborah!" he called as he strode toward her, afraid he would lose her once more.

She turned toward him, and her face lit with pleasure. "What a surprise to see you here."

"Hello, Edward. I'm often here of a Thursday."

"Indeed?"

"Yes. I would like you to meet Thomas Crowe. He assists me." She turned to the boy. "Thomas, this is Mr. Hunter."

The boy stared at him as Edward held out his hand and said, "Pleased to meet you." After a moment, Thomas shook his hand, then quickly withdrew it.

"Er. . .assists you with what, if I may ask?"

"With making my purchases."

Edward frowned and eyed the basket on her arm, then studied the larger one the boy was carrying. Surely the Bowmans had servants to do their shopping for them, and he doubted their household would need yams and tea in such quantities.

"This is a rowdy place for a lady, especially when a ship has newly docked. We get all sorts of people in here, Deborah."

She smiled. "I know it. That's part of what Thomas is for. Mother forbade me to come by myself."

"I still don't quite. . . ." He looked pointedly at her heaped basket. "I mean, that's a lot of tea."

"Yes, it is."

He was at a loss for words, and she laughed at his expression.

"I see I shall have to educate you about my Thursday outings. But it's noisy in here. Perhaps you can visit the house another time, and we can discuss it."

Delight sprang up in his heart at her suggestion, but it was quickly followed by a thud of disappointment.

"I'm afraid I must decline that enticing offer."

"Oh?" She was clearly disappointed as well, and he was somewhat gratified.

"Now that the *Prosper* is in, Jacob wants me to leave immediately for Portsmouth to see about buying that other ship we mentioned."

"The *Resolute*," she said.

"Yes." It shouldn't surprise him that she remembered. "Please believe me, I would much rather spend the time in your parlor discussing your Thursday schedule or any other topic to your liking, but Jacob is right; if we don't act quickly, we'll lose this chance. In fact, we've already delayed action several weeks on this matter, and the *Resolute* may already be sold to someone else."

"Of course you must go," she said.

He nodded. "Thank you for understanding. I shall leave at high tide in the morning, and I expect to be gone several days, perhaps a week."

Her eyes seemed to lose a little of their glow, and he knew he had let her down. But she shook her head and smiled up at him. "Then we shall have to meet when you return. I'll pray you have a safe journey."

"Thank you." He hesitated, then looked at the boy again. "Er. . ."

"Oh, the provisions. You see, a couple of years ago, I began a service of sorts that occupies me on Thursdays."

"A service?"

"Yes. In the past, your father always allowed me to buy a few staples at wholesale each week or anytime a ship came in."

Edward was puzzled by this, but by now he knew that, Deborah being Deborah, she probably had a good reason.

She laughed. "I see that I shall have to tell you my secret in full. Just, please, don't spread it about, will you? It threatens their dignity."

"Whose?"

"The sailors' wives. Or widows, I should say."

"You are taking food to sailors' widows?"

"A little food and a great deal of conversation and company. That's what I do best."

"And my mother is one of your ladies?"

Her merry grin at that warmed him to his toes.

"No, your mother is in a special class by herself. She often helps me in my cause by donating clothing and foodstuffs. But you see, by obtaining food, clothing, and other goods at wholesale prices from the city's traders, I am able to help several families. . . . Well, to be plain, I help them survive."

Edward drew a deep breath. Deborah *would* undertake a cause like that. She saw a need in the seaside city, and instead of petitioning the community's leaders to meet it, she endeavored to help those she could.

"How many families?"

"I've given small aid to about a dozen so far."

"And the boy is part of this?" he asked.

Deborah flashed her smile toward Thomas. "He is the son of a brave man who died at sea."

"I'll soon be old enough to sail myself, sir," Thomas said. "But my mother wants me at home for now."

Edward could understand that. If the husband was lost, the wife would be slow to let her children take up the sailor's life.

"Each week he helps me carry the goods I buy to his mother's house, where I distribute them," Deborah said.

Edward nodded. He was seeing a new side of Deborah, and his impression of her sweet compassion combined with her energy and practical good sense only grew more defined.

"I'm glad my father promoted your efforts."

"Thank you. Your uncle let me continue to come here after Mr. Hunter died. I hope you don't mind. I probably should have asked you."

"No, that's fine. In fact. . ." He glanced toward where he had left Jacob, but his cousin was gone, no doubt into the office to set up the delivery and fees for transporting Engle's lumber. "In fact, I'd like to give you a load of provisions for these families. Just tell me what is needed, and I'll have a wagonload delivered."

Deborah opened her mouth, swallowed, then found her voice. "Thank you, that's very generous. But you can hardly do that every week, or you would lose money. What I usually do is go around and solicit private donations from my friends and some of the business owners in town. If you are willing to let me continue buying at wholesale, that is enough."

"But surely you have ladies who need more than tea and"— he peered into Thomas's basket—"and sugar. Let me this once give you a wagon full."

"Well. . ." She tilted her head toward her shoulder, considering.

Edward's heart leaped, and he longed to throw his arms around her. In that moment, he knew that life without Deborah would be boring and flat. In her world, there would never be a day without some joy, or at least the satisfaction of a worthy effort completed. That was a life he wanted to share.

"Perhaps a few things," she agreed. "Mrs. Lewis has a baby and could use some soft flannel. I hadn't looked at the yard goods yet."

"Yes! You shall have a bolt of flannel and one of calico. And some rice and coffee and all the salt fish and molasses you can use. And from now on, when you come to the warehouse to buy for your ladies, you will buy at cost."

"At cost?"

"My cost, not wholesale."

"Oh, Edward, you'll bankrupt yourself."

"Nonsense. You won't put a nick in all this." He waved his arm, encompassing the whole warehouse and almost hitting a merchant who was passing.

She hesitated, then nodded. "I shan't say no. Thank you."

He smiled. "That's fine. Pick out what you want today. And

fill the wagon. I mean it. This day's goods are my gift to you and the families. I'll have one of the men drive the wagon around to the place where you distribute the lot."

"That would be the Crowe residence." She named a street in the poorest section of town.

He nodded, keeping his face straight so as not to embarrass the boy, but the thought of Deborah going there appalled him.

"I'll send a good man to drive the wagon and help unload when you get there. Will you ride on the wagon seat with him?"

"Oh no, Thomas and I shall walk."

"Do you. . .walk down there often?"

"Every week unless Abby goes with me. Then we take a hack."

He stood speechless for a moment. The thought of Abby joining this enterprise shocked him, but with persuasion from the earnest Deborah, he supposed even that was possible. His admiration for Deborah and his longing to be with her urged him to make a further overture. He drew a careful breath and reached for her arm, turning her slightly away from the boy.

"I was wondering," Edward said.

"Yes?"

"When I come back from Portsmouth, may I call on you?"

"You can visit my family anytime."

"No, I mean *you*, Deborah."

She caught her breath and looked away, staring off toward the open door of the warehouse, where clerks were totaling up a buyer's purchases and accepting payment.

"Deborah?"

"Mm?" Her face was crimson, but she turned toward him and raised her chin until her melting brown eyes looked into his face.

"If you'll permit it, I'd like to come next week to call on you. What do you say?"

She opened her mouth, but nothing came out. Was she

wondering what Abigail would say? Or perhaps what her father's reaction would be?

She swallowed and tried again. "I would be delighted."

Edward smiled. "Then I shall look forward to it during my voyage to Portsmouth. Now, speak for your merchandise, and I'll arrange for the wagon."

She thanked him again and turned away. Edward watched her for a moment as she headed for the bolts of material in search of soft flannel for babies' diapers. He ought to insist that she stay out of that part of town.

He almost laughed at himself. She'd been doing this for two years while he had been off digging clams and carving sticks to kill time on Spring Island. And Abigail sometimes went with her! Unbelievable! He still couldn't picture Abby entering the humble huts of the sailors' widows. But Deborah. . . Yes, he could see her doing it.

Suddenly he wanted to hurry through the rest of this day. He wanted to put the voyage to Portsmouth behind him and come home quickly. Home to Deborah.

twelve

"It's got to be the tonnage," Edward said, frowning over the mass of papers he had spread across his desk. "Nothing else makes any sense."

"How so?" Jacob asked. He shuffled through the manifests, logs, and sales reports, looking a bit lost.

"On her last few voyages, the total cargo on the *Prosper* was a lower volume than capacity."

"Really? I didn't notice that." Jacob pushed aside one of the ledgers and picked up another sheet of paper.

"It wasn't much off, but on her first voyage last year, the cargo totaled up less tonnage than you'd expect. Then, on the second trip, when she docked last fall, there seems to have been a shortage again, unless I'm missing something. Take a look at the manifest. They could easily have loaded more coffee or molasses in the Indies."

Jacob sat down and puzzled over the papers Edward had indicated.

"But this doesn't prove that anything's amiss."

"Not in itself," Edward agreed. "But this latest cargo. . ."

"Oh, really, Ed." Jacob looked up at him with troubled eyes. "You helped unload her yourself. They had that ship filled to the gunwales."

He nodded, mulling it over in his mind. "Yes, but with what? You've told me several times you expected several tons of coffee to come in. Stuart brought us only a small supply. We could have sold ten times as much coffee today. But this cargo was heavy on rice and raw cotton, Jake. Products we don't make much on when we resell them."

Jacob pressed his lips together and inhaled, looking down

at the papers once more. "Captain Stuart told me he got all he could. Should we have him in tomorrow and question him further about this?"

Edward frowned and sat on the corner of his desk. "I'm not sure. I've read his log, and though there's nothing obviously wrong there, it seems a bit vague in spots. He said they turned back for repairs at one point, but the time spent on what should have been a minor job doesn't fit." He stood up. "Let's talk to some of the other men."

Jacob smiled. "Jamie Sibley. He was on the *Egret* with us, remember?"

"Aye."

"He was always a good lad. I put him on the sloop last year, but for this current voyage, I made him the *Prosper*'s second mate."

"Perfect," said Edward. "He was with you in the *Egret*'s yawl."

"Yes. I wouldn't question his loyalty to me or Hunter Shipping."

Edward nodded, liking it more and more. "Let's go."

As they walked the quiet streets of the harbor, Edward's mind surged with questions. They came to the corner of the street where the Sibley family lived, and he paused.

"Jacob, I hope you'll forgive me, but I had to start at the top on this. I've been looking pretty hard at you and Mr. Daniels the past few weeks."

"At me and—oh, Ed."

"Yes, well, I had to be sure. At first I wasn't even certain anything was going on. But I'm sure now. You had nothing to do with it, though."

Jacob's hurt expression pierced him.

"Can you forgive me for doubting you?"

"Well, I suppose you had to. I mean, it's your company and your family. Abby, too. You had to be sure she wasn't marrying a rapscallion."

"Yes. But still. . . Well, I never really thought you could do something like that to Hunter Shipping. Why would you, after all, when it looked as though you'd end up with the whole business? But there were enough indicators to make me look over all the men in the office."

"Father, too, I suppose." Jacob bowed his head, and Edward wished he could deny it; however, the truth was he'd thought of Uncle Felix, too, and whether or not there was some way he could have shorted the company when cargoes came into the warehouse.

"I. . .decided he wouldn't do that, and anyway, the discrepancies originate with the bills of lading and manifests, I believe. This thievery has taken place before the ship docks; that's my belief."

Jacob nodded.

"I'd have taken you into my confidence sooner, but. . .well, as you say, I had to be certain." Edward extended his hand. "We're in this together now, and it feels good to have an ally at my back."

Jacob grasped his hand. "I'm here for you. Let's see what Jamie has to say."

The *Prosper*'s second mate left his family at dinner and joined them in the yard of the small house.

"Mr. Hunter. Mr. Price. How can I help you gents?" He eyed them uneasily.

"We're sorry to disturb you, Jamie," Jacob said with a smile. "My cousin and I just had a few questions we'd like to ask about your voyage. Nothing to worry about."

"It's my fault," Edward said. "As you know, I've been away for a while."

"Yes, sir," Jamie replied. "And glad I was to hear you was alive."

Edward nodded. "Thank you. Mr. Price has told me how you helped the men of the *Egret*'s yawl survive, and I believe he used good judgment in promoting you."

Jamie glanced at Jacob, then shuffled his feet, looking down as he pushed a pebble about with his toe. "Thank you, sir. I was glad for the opportunity."

"Well, I'm leaving tomorrow on a short trip in the company's sloop," Edward said. "Going to Portsmouth. You wouldn't like to go along, would you? I'll be looking at another schooner we're thinking of buying."

Jamie's face lit up. "Oh, yes, sir, I'd be privileged to make that run. And say, if you's buying another ship, will there be berths on her for a new voyage?"

"Tired of the *Prosper*?" Jacob asked.

Jamie looked down at his feet again. "She's a good ship, sir, but. . .I'd just as soon try something new."

Jacob reached out and touched the young man's shoulder. "Jamie, we've been through a lot together, and I know you'll be honest with me. Is something slippery going on with the *Prosper*?"

Jamie exhaled sharply and glanced Edward's way, then looked back to Jacob. "It started with the coffee."

"Coffee?"

Edward kept quiet and let Jacob continue the interview, since Jamie Sibley obviously felt more comfortable with him.

"Yes, sir, we took on a prodigious supply in Jamaica. Finest Brazilian coffee, they had. More than half our cargo."

Jacob cocked his head to one side. "But, Jamie, when we unloaded yesterday and today. . ."

Jamie nodded, his forehead furrowed with wrinkles. "I know, I know. But Captain Stuart. . ."

"What?" Jacob asked.

"Well, sir. . ."

They waited a long moment.

"We went to St. Augustine and off-loaded most of the coffee, sir."

"You sold the coffee in Florida?" Jacob shot Edward a glance, but Edward kept still.

"Y—yes, sir. I wasn't sure what was going on, but I supposed the captain had orders from you. After that, we headed south again, and that's when I heard him telling Mr. Rankin—"

"The first mate," Jacob said to Edward, and Jamie nodded.

"Yes, sir. I heard him tell Mr. Rankin we'd run back down there quick and fill up with coffee again, and. . .and none would be the wiser, sir."

"Meaning me, I suppose." Jacob shook his head. "It's true, then. Ed, I'm not as sharp as you are with figures, and the whole thing slipped past me. He's selling off part of the cargo and reloading afterward. That's why it took Stuart so long to get back here this voyage."

"Aye," said Jamie. "But when we got back to Jamaica, they had hardly any coffee left. The captain was in a black mood. We pushed on to Havana, but he couldn't get any there, either. We couldn't go all the way to Rio for it, so we took on cotton and rice and whatever else he could get."

Edward took a deep breath. "I suppose something similar happened on her two voyages last year?"

Jamie shrugged. "I wasn't on board then, sir, but yes, from what the other fellows have told me, I'd think so. They sold off a bit of the most expensive goods at some other port."

"And the captain thought they'd all keep quiet?" Jacob asked.

Jamie hesitated. "Well, sir, he gave out there'd be something extra in it for them, and he told me. . . . Well, he told me he'd give me something later, but I must keep mum about the extra dealings." He threw an uneasy glance at Edward. "I'm sorry. I been fretting on it these two days since we docked, thinking I ought to come and tell you gents. You coming here. . . Well, that tipped it for me. I should have come to you sooner."

Jacob clapped his shoulder. "All's forgiven, Jamie, so long as you understand you're siding with us now."

"We'll turn this over to the law," Edward added. "You might be needed to testify."

Jamie swallowed hard. "It won't sit well with the men."

"We'll get you out of here tomorrow on the sloop with Mr. Hunter," Jacob said. "I'll go to see the magistrate, and I won't mention your name unless it's necessary. When you come back from Portsmouth, you might need to write out a statement or some such."

"Somebody'd have to write it for me, sir."

Jacob nodded. "Yes, well, don't you worry, Jamie. When we're done, Captain Stuart won't be able to get another ship, and any man who's been in this with him will face the law as well."

"That amounts to the whole crew, sir." Jamie seemed appalled at what his confession had put in motion.

Edward said, "We'll bring the men in and question them, and any who own up and give evidence against the captain will be kept on."

Jamie sighed. "Thank you, sir. There's some as weren't even smart enough to catch on, and then there's some who was just scared of the captain and Mr. Rankin."

Edward nodded. "We'll take that into consideration. Now go back to your family and rest easy tonight, Jamie. Be on the wharf at dawn, and we'll sail for Portsmouth."

Edward and Jacob walked silently up the street and out of the harbor district.

"Can you handle things tomorrow?" Edward asked at last.

"I believe I can," Jacob said. "I'll take Mr. Daniels into my confidence and go around to the magistrate first thing."

Edward nodded. "Perhaps your father could help you question the sailors. They're all afraid of him, and he could put the fear of the law into most of those boys."

Jacob smiled. "That's a thought."

"If you want me to stay. . ."

"No. You take Jamie and go see about that ship. Now that we know what's been going on with the *Prosper*, there's no reason we can't add the *Resolute* to the fleet and press forward."

❧

Deborah knocked on the door of the Hunter house and looked around as she waited. The garden was a riot of color. She knew Mrs. Hunter employed three servants to keep the house and grounds in order. It was the Tuesday between her usual visits for tea, and Deborah wondered if her hostess had invited her so she could show her the lovely gardens in bloom.

Jenny opened the door and smiled. "Hello, Miss Deborah. Mrs. Hunter has a lady with her in the sitting room."

"Oh, I beg your pardon," Deborah said. "I'll come back another day."

"No, no. She insisted I bring you right in." Jenny opened the door wide and motioned her inside, so Deborah entered and handed her a basket.

"A few late strawberries for Mrs. Hunter."

"Oh, she'll be pleased. Go right in, won't you?"

Deborah removed her gloves, wondering if she'd been invited on purpose to meet the other guest. Timidly she peered into the small room. Mrs. Hunter spied her at once and stood to greet her.

"Come in, come in." To the other woman in the room, she said, "This is Miss Bowman, the physician's daughter, an old acquaintance who has lately become a good friend of mine."

The other woman did not stand but accepted Deborah's hand. She was about fifty, Deborah supposed, and elegantly dressed in a tan silk day dress edged in deep, ruffled flounces. The lady looked her over sharply, giving her the feeling that she was under inspection. Her feathered hat drooped over one ear and set off her stylishly curled hair.

"How do you do," Deborah said.

"Bowman," the woman murmured. Louder, she said, "Are you the young woman who threw Edward Hunter over for his cousin?"

Deborah felt her face go scarlet. Mrs. Hunter also flushed.

Her only aid to Deborah's discomfiture was an apologetic smile.

"Actually," Deborah said, releasing the lady's hand, "that would be my sister, Abigail. I am Deborah."

The lady nodded. "I see."

"Deborah, this is Mrs. King," Edward's mother said.

"Mrs. . ." Deborah gulped and used her selection of a chair as an excuse not to meet the lady's eyes for a moment, while she grappled for her composure. *I've just been introduced to the governor's wife. Was I rude? Oh dear, I hope not! But she was rude first.* She swallowed again, gathered her skirts, sat down, and smiled.

"Let me give you your tea." Mrs. Hunter poured out a cup for her, and Deborah accepted it, suddenly conscious of the dark stains under her nails left by the many strawberries she'd hulled that morning for her mother's preserve making.

"Thank you."

"So your sister is the foolish chit who gave young Mr. Hunter the mitten?"

Mrs. Hunter smiled at her guests. "It's really for the best, you know, Ann. They were so young when Edward went to sea, and then he was away for five years. They both had time to mature while he was gone. And when he came back, they found they'd outgrown their childish infatuation."

Deborah tried to hold her smile but felt it slipping. This was too humiliating.

Mrs. King didn't seem to think so. "Well, I still say she missed a good opportunity. Of course, I haven't met her new intended groom. But I have met Edward, and any girl who would—"

"I'm surprised you heard about it all the way up in Bath," Mrs. Hunter said.

"We hear everything," Mrs. King stated. "Of course, my husband is in Portland much of the time now. We're taking a house here until his term is up. That's why I'm with him on this trip, you know. We're only staying at the Robisons' home until the place we're leasing is cleaned and our baggage arrives."

"How lovely," said Mrs. Hunter. "Your husband does need to be here in the thick of things just now."

"Yes. He's had many social invitations and no way to return them, so I'll be setting up housekeeping and scheduling some affairs."

"I'm so pleased that you had time to come and spend the afternoon with me," Mrs. Hunter said.

"Well, I enjoy getting out and about, and I always make time for old friends. I was hoping to see Edward, though. We've heard so much about his death-defying feat. Do you expect him home today?"

"I'm not sure." Mrs. Hunter glanced at Deborah with an inclusive smile. "Edward ran down the coast in the company's sloop a few days ago, but he should be back soon. I've asked the gentlemen at the office to send me a note the minute he returns."

"How do you dare let him go off again so soon?" Mrs. King shook her head and sipped her tea.

"It's only to Portsmouth, and I'm not worried about Edward. He's proven himself well able to survive even the most unfavorable circumstances. Isn't that right, Deborah?"

"Oh. . .yes, certainly. He's a very capable sailor."

"I suppose you have a point," Mrs. King said. "I'm so glad my husband doesn't sail on his ships, though. William sends them off full of apples and potatoes and lumber, and they come back filled with cotton and coal."

"How expedient," Mrs. Hunter said.

Deborah was startled when her hostess winked at her. Apparently Mrs. Hunter had the same thought she did—that the life Mrs. King led must be boring.

"Yes, well, the general has enough to do without floating around the globe. He was hoping to see your son, though.

He tells me he's been meaning to call here since he heard of Edward's return but hasn't found time. So busy, with the new legislature meeting and all."

"Your husband is welcome anytime," Mrs. Hunter assured her. "Of course, Edward would be happy to see him and tell him of his misadventure. Perhaps we can have dinner here once we know what Edward's schedule will be."

"Good, good. That would be most pleasant. I hope to arrange some small dinner parties in the new house. It's a bit cramped, so large gatherings would be awkward. But there are a good many statesmen and merchants who've entertained General King over the past few months, and I simply must reciprocate to them and their wives. That will be my first order of business once we're settled."

"I'm sure the entire city looks forward to it," her hostess said. "Your affairs are always delightful. Now, Deborah, I do wish you'd tell me about your Thursday project. How are things going, dear?"

Deborah had relaxed, glad to be ignored, and she flinched when Mrs. Hunter drew attention to her again. "Very well, thank you."

She saw Mrs. King's inquisitive look and was about to explain her widows' aid endeavor when Jenny appeared in the doorway.

"Yes, Jenny, what is it?" Mrs. Hunter asked.

"The apprentice brought a note, ma'am, from the office."

"Oh, thank you."

Jenny handed her a folded sheet of paper, and Mrs. Hunter quickly opened it and scanned the contents. Deborah watched her face, unable to suppress an anxious stirring in her stomach. Had she been truthful when she agreed that she did not worry about Edward?

His mother smiled. "Captain Moody has raised a flag indicating he has spotted a vessel flying Hunter Shipping's colors approaching the harbor. This note is from Mr. Price, saying they are preparing a berth on the wharf."

"The *Resolute*?" Deborah breathed.

"I don't know, dear." Mrs. Hunter's eyes glittered with inspiration. "Say, why don't we go down to the wharf and see?"

"Go to the docks?" Mrs. King's arched eyebrows and shocked tone told Deborah the governor's wife did not approve of the enterprise.

"We'll take a carriage," Mrs. Hunter went on. "If Edward has come home again, this time he shall have folks to welcome him when he steps ashore."

"Marvelous!" Deborah clapped her hands together, glad that Mrs. Hunter was undaunted.

"But the docks," Mrs. King said. "Is it safe, my dear?"

"Of course." Mrs. Hunter reached for the bell pull. "The men on Hunter's Wharf all know me and respect my husband's memory."

As Jenny came to the door, Mrs. King stood and reached for her reticule. "I fear I must go back to the Robisons' house. We'll be dining out tonight, and I must catch a nap. Our journey here quite fatigued me."

"We'll drop you off on our way to the wharf." Mrs. Hunter's animated face fed Deborah's excitement. Edward was returning, and she would be on hand to greet him. Her parents would not object since she would be in the company of his mother.

"Jenny, send Mercer to bring a hack. We three ladies are going out."

thirteen

"Aunt Mary! So glad to see you today." Jacob opened the door of the hired carriage and gave Mrs. Hunter his hand. "And Deborah! Welcome."

"Thank you," Deborah said as she lifted her skirt and stepped carefully down.

"Come. I've brought my spyglass, and we can walk out past the store and have a good view down the river."

"Do you know yet what vessel it is?" Mrs. Hunter puffed as they walked the length of the long pier, but she would not allow Jacob to slacken the pace.

"Not for certain, but I think it's still too early for the *Falcon*." They stood together waiting. Jacob turned his spyglass toward Captain Moody's tower.

"One of our ships. I haven't called many laborers in because we're not expecting to unload a cargo today. Although Edward might have picked up a few bundles in Portsmouth."

A sharp-eyed lad gave a whoop and waved toward the mouth of the Fore. Deborah squinted and saw a vessel pull out from behind the headland of Cape Elizabeth. It was too small for the schooner they'd hoped to see.

"That's our sloop." Jacob's voice drooped in disappointment. "Well, Edward's likely on board, so your trip is not wasted."

"I did hope we'd get a first glimpse of the company's new ship," Mrs. Hunter said. "Ah well, perhaps it wasn't all we'd hoped, and he passed on buying it."

"Or perhaps she was already sold." Jacob held the spyglass out to Deborah. "Would you like to take a look?"

"Thank you." She trained the lens on the distant sloop, searching its deck for a tall, broad-shouldered man whose

133

dark hair whipped in the wind. None of the sailors she saw had Edward's stature or bearing.

She offered the glass to Mrs. Hunter. "Would you care to look?"

"Oh yes. Thanks, dear." Mrs. Hunter scanned the sloop. "I don't see Edward."

"Nor did I," said Deborah.

His mother turned and studied the observatory tower through the spyglass.

"Jacob."

"Yes, Aunt Mary?"

"Captain Moody's run up another signal."

"Oh?"

Mrs. Hunter handed him the spyglass, and Jacob turned to look toward the tower on Munjoy Hill.

"You're right!" Excitement fired his voice.

Deborah shaded her eyes with her hand and tried to make out the distant flag.

"It's our colors again. Either the *Falcon*'s come home in record time, or Edward's bought the *Resolute*."

They all waited as the sloop drew nearer, the wind carrying her against the current. As the vessel came in closer, Deborah could make out half-a-dozen men on the deck, bustling to make the mooring.

"Ahoy, Sibley!" Jacob cried to the man who seemed to be directing them. "Where's Mr. Hunter?"

"Yonder!" Sibley motioned behind him, down the river.

Deborah could hardly contain her excitement. Jacob handed her the spyglass and scurried to help tie up the sloop. She put the brass tube to her eye and focused on the point of land where the sloop had first appeared.

Empty water lay restless between the shores.

Suddenly a dark bulk poked into her circle of vision.

"There she is!" Mrs. Hunter cried.

Deborah lowered the spyglass. Far away but coming about

toward them, a majestic ship under sail hove into sight. Deborah drew a sharp breath. "She's beautiful!"

"Magnificent. Larger than Mr. King's flagship, too."

Deborah chuckled at Mrs. Hunter's satisfied smile. She handed over the spyglass and watched the ship as the crew went aloft, ready to take in canvas.

"I see him!" Mrs. Hunter bounced on her toes. "He's standing amidships just under the mainsail. Look, Deborah! He's waving his hat."

The next half hour sped past as the *Resolute* settled into her new berth at the outer end of Hunter's Wharf. The gangplank was put in place, and Jacob led the ladies onto the deck.

Edward met them at the rail, grinning like a child who'd found a half dime, and assisted them in descending to the deck.

"Do you like her?" he shouted to Jacob, who hopped down on his own power.

"She's perfect! Everything Smith told me and more."

"And the best part is she's in wondrous shape. There's hardly anything to be done before we can put her to sea. She handles like a dream, Jake!"

Edward smiled down at Deborah, and she realized he was still holding her gloved hand. She pulled it away reluctantly.

"Oh, Ed, about that matter we discussed the evening before you left," Jacob said.

Deborah watched curiously as Edward sobered. "All went well?"

"Yes, things are in hand, and when the sloop docked, I told Jamie he has no cause to worry."

"And Stuart?" Edward asked.

"Justice is in motion. I'll tell you all about it later, but things are proceeding as we hoped."

Edward nodded. "That's good, then. Well, Mother, what do you think of the *Resolute*?"

"Makes me wish I were younger," Mrs. Hunter said, surveying the deck and the rigging. "I'd ask you to take me on her next voyage and relive the old days."

"You've been to sea?" Deborah asked.

"Oh yes. When my husband and I were first married, I took two voyages with him. It's something I remember fondly, though there were frightening moments. All in all, being with the captain and understanding his love of sailing was valuable to our marriage. And seeing other places and people so different from us New Englanders opened my eyes. I've never looked at folks the same since."

"I should like to make such a trip." Deborah sighed, then realized Edward was watching her.

"Perhaps you shall someday," he said.

She felt her face color and was alarmed when he took her arm and led her a few steps away from the others.

"I should like to come round this evening to call on you, if I may."

"Of course." A thought suddenly struck her. "Oh, Edward, I haven't told Father."

He sobered. "Do you think he'll object?"

"Why no, I don't think so."

"Fine, then, I'll ask him. When will he be at home?"

She glanced around him and saw his mother carrying on a spirited conversation with Jacob as they walked toward the stairs leading up to the quarterdeck.

"By six, if his patients don't keep him. He's usually home for dinner."

"Good, I'll take dinner at home, then come around and see your father. If all is to his liking, we'll have some time together afterward."

Deborah felt her mouth go dry. She'd never been courted before, but she had no doubt that was Edward's intention.

"I. . .we. . ."

"Yes?" Edward's eyes twinkled as he gazed down at her.

"We may have to compete for space in the parlor with your cousin and Abby."

Edward laughed, and her heart lifted. "Have they set a date yet?"

"Yes. The eighteenth of August."

"Well, we'll turn the tables on them. You chaperoned your sister many an evening, and now it's her turn."

Deborah's heart skipped. Never in her life had she been in need of a chaperone, but a quick glance at Edward's gleaming dark eyes told her the time had come. Perhaps her mother would stop despairing of ever seeing her married. That thought was enough to send an anticipatory shiver through her.

Edward reached for her hands and squeezed them. "You blush most becomingly. Come. I'm supposed to be showing off my new schooner, and poor Jacob has had to haul Mother off so I could have a private word with you."

"Is that what he's doing?"

"Of course. But we'd better relieve him and let him get on with his official duties. He and Mr. Daniels will have some paperwork to do. We'll have to register the ship and decide what we want for crew and cargo for her first voyage under Hunter Shipping's colors." He pulled Deborah's hand through the crook of his arm and took her toward the companionway that led above, where Jacob and Mrs. Hunter were now inspecting the tiller.

"Where will she sail?" Deborah asked.

"To the Indies, I think, unless Jacob has a full cargo waiting to be taken to some other place. Oh, they're coming down. I'll show you all the captain's cabin. It's quite spacious for the size of the ship."

"Would you captain her yourself?" Deborah asked.

"I might. Bringing her up from Portsmouth was a joy. I wouldn't mind going out again on her."

"What?" his mother barked, descending the last steps. "Did you say you're leaving again?"

"No, Mother. I merely said that with a deck like this one under his feet, a man feels like sailing."

"You're not going to hire a captain to handle this ship for you?"

"Of course we are," Jacob said, scowling at Edward. "I have several names. There are good men out there waiting for a ship."

Edward smiled. "Then I expect we'll get someone, Mother. We haven't had time to discuss any of that yet."

She looked at him, then down the length of the main deck. "She is a lovely vessel. I wouldn't blame you a bit if you wanted to sail her. But don't forget your family."

"I won't. Now come and see the captain's quarters. Whoever he may be, the master of this ship will be quite comfortable."

Deborah sighed as she viewed the neat cabin. Mrs. Hunter spun round on the carpeted floor, exclaiming over the polished wood of the built-in cupboards and drawers, the folding table, the curtained bunk, and the mullioned window in the stern of the ship.

"Oh, if we'd had a cabin like this on the *Hermia*, I'd have been the happiest bride on earth. As it was, we had a tiny room one-third this size, and your father insisted on keeping his trunk in the cabin. We could barely turn around and were always tripping over that chest."

Edward laughed. "I'll keep that in mind, Mother, if I ever ask a woman to share a cabin with me." He winked at Deborah, and she felt her blush shoot all the way to the tips of her ears.

❧

"What shall I do if Father isn't home before Edward arrives?" Deborah threw an anxious glance at Abigail in the mirror as her sister brushed out her thick, dark hair.

"We'll just have a pleasant evening with two gentlemen callers, and Edward can speak to him tomorrow. Don't fret so."

Deborah smiled at Abby's reflection. "I'm not fretting."

"Yes you are. You haven't been still for ten seconds since you sat down."

Deborah was surprised that her wayward tresses were obedient to Abby's gentle coaxing and lay in gentle waves about her forehead.

"Do you like it?" Abigail asked.

"I'm not sure. It doesn't look like me."

"Well, it's time you started paying more attention to your looks. You're very pretty, you know. If you'd dress up a little and guard your complexion from the sun, the young men would hang about our doorstep in droves."

"Not true."

"Well, at least half true. You'd have to stop treating them like chums as well."

"And how should I treat them?"

"Like fascinating men."

"Most of them are boring."

"You seem to find Edward interesting."

Deborah whirled around in dismay. "Does it upset you that he asked to come calling on me so soon after. . .after your decision?"

Abigail smiled and shook her head, patting at a stubborn strand of hair over Deborah's ear. "Why should that bother me? I have the man I want."

"Oh, Abby, it wasn't my intention to attract him."

"I know."

"Then why do I feel so awful?"

"No reason. You should feel pleased and honored. Edward is a fine man, as you've told me many times."

Deborah puzzled over her sister's serenity. "You seem so calm now, but a few weeks ago you were overwrought."

"Because I knew I loved Jacob and couldn't bear to hurt Edward. I couldn't help but wonder if it was my duty to marry him, even though it would rip my heart to shreds. But now, seeing that he's accepted the outcome, I feel much easier."

"You don't think it's horrid of him to want to pay attention to me so soon?"

Abigail's smile had a wise twist that Deborah had never seen before. "I expect that if I hadn't become attached to Jacob before Edward came home we still would have found eventually that we were not perfectly suited to each other."

"Really?"

"Yes. It might have taken us months to discover that, however. You see, God works things out."

Deborah nodded. "I'm sorry I was cross with you."

"You had a right to be. I didn't behave very well at first. But I also think that you and Edward have an admiration for one another that transcends the years of his absence."

"You do?"

Abby reached for a hairpin. "Mm-hmm. You know you've always adored him."

"Yes, I have. But he only saw me as your bother of a little sister."

"Perhaps, but he commented to me several times in the old days about how clever you were and what a beauty you would make some day."

The air Deborah gulped felt like a square lump.

"I never, ever thought he'd think of me as. . .a woman."

Abigail laughed and squeezed her shoulder. "You're so droll, Debbie. It's quite a relief to me that Edward's not crushed. It would have been miserable to see him at church and social functions for the rest of my life, with him slouching about and staring at me with those huge, dark eyes."

"Edward wouldn't do such a thing."

"Perhaps not, but he does have a melancholy tendency. You are just what he needs. I predict you'll keep him in high spirits. I never should have accomplished that."

Deborah started to protest, but Abigail picked up another hairpin. "Turn around and let me finish.

The image in the mirror stared back at Deborah with dark,

anxious eyes. Her sister's skillful ministrations had brought her hair into a soft, becoming style. Would Edward think she was pretty?

"Thank you, Abby. I confess I'm a bit nervous."

"Well, you shouldn't be. You're much more suited to him in temperament than I ever was." Abigail tugged at her sleeve. "Stand up now. I think the red shawl will set off that white gown splendidly."

"Oh no, the red is too bright." Deborah already felt misgivings at wearing the new white dress. The neck, while not daring, was lower than she was accustomed to, and she feared her blush would become perpetual.

"It is not," Abigail insisted, holding up the shawl in question. "Red is all the fashion, and it goes very well with the delicate flower pattern of your gown."

"No, I think I'd better wear my gray shawl."

"Impossible. I'm wearing it." Abigail seized Deborah's usual dove gray wrap and threw it over her own shoulders. "It goes well with my green dress, don't you think?"

"Well. . ."

"Come on." Abigail took her hand and sidestepped toward the door. "I heard the knocker. Jacob's probably cooling his heels and waiting for his dinner."

fourteen

Edward arrived at the Bowman house amid a gray drizzle that brought an early dusk. The family was just leaving the dinner table. They had delayed the meal, hoping Dr. Bowman could join them, Deborah told him.

"Father was detained with a patient this evening," she explained.

Edward's disappointment at being unable to settle his business with the doctor was short-lived. The shy, hopeful smile she bestowed on him made all obstacles shrink.

"Ah. Then we shall pass a pleasant evening in spite of his absence, and perhaps I can have a word with him tomorrow."

Mrs. Bowman carried into the parlor a tray bearing coffee and a bowl of sugared walnuts. The young people settled down, with Abigail and Jacob on the sofa and Deborah and Edward in chairs opposite them, while Mrs. Bowman sat in the cushioned rocker near the hearth.

"It's chilly this evening," she said. "This rain."

"Would you like a fire, ma'am?" Edward asked. "I can kindle it for you."

"A fire in the parlor in July?" Mrs. Bowman shook her head.

"Must we be so frugal, Mother?" Abigail asked. "It's cold, and the fire's already laid for just such a night."

"All right, then." Mrs. Bowman edged her chair back to give Edward room to work. He pulled the painted fire screen aside, and soon a comforting blaze threw its warmth to them all.

They spent two hours in enjoyable conversation, mostly concerning the new government and the upcoming wedding. Mrs. Bowman seemed hesitant to discuss the latter topic when Abigail first brought it up, casting worried looks in Edward's direction.

He smiled, hoping to put her at ease. "My cousin has invited me to stand up with him for the ceremony. I'm looking forward to performing that duty."

After that, Mrs. Bowman relaxed and brought out her sewing. Deborah began to knit, glancing up only now and then.

"And Deborah shall have a new gown as well," Abigail said. "Lavender, I think. We're going to shop for material tomorrow."

"The one she's wearing now suits her admirably," Edward said.

Abigail smiled. "Isn't it lovely on her? But I want her to have something a little fancier. Mother, too."

Deborah stared at her knitting, her lips firmly closed. He supposed that hearing her appearance discussed was not at all to her liking, though he was pleased he'd had a chance to let her know he approved. Her hair was different tonight. Softer somehow, and it suited her sweet features.

"Really, dear. People don't make so much of a wedding," Mrs. Bowman said.

"No, but it's for the party afterward." Abigail laughed. "All the best people will come, and the women, at least, will be lavishly turned out. Why, Father said we may even invite Governor and Mrs. King."

"Oh dear," Deborah muttered.

"And, Edward," Abigail went on, turning a brilliant smile on him, "you must know your mother has offered her garden and parlors for the affair."

"Very gracious of her," said her mother. "We'd haven't much space here, but Mrs. Hunter insisted we hold a reception there for the young people."

"So she's told me," Edward said. "After all, Jacob is her favorite nephew."

Jacob chuckled. "Aunt Mary is quite excited about it. She and Mother are having a grand time planning the menu."

"She wanted to serve dinner for forty, but we told her that was too much for her," Abigail said.

"Oh, I don't know. She surprises me with her energy these days." Edward shook his head. "I think she does more entertaining now than she did when Father was alive."

"Her gardens are so beautiful that I could not refuse," Mrs. Bowman told him. "Most kind of her. Abigail and I are going over tomorrow afternoon after we finish our shopping to make plans with her and Mrs. Price."

Deborah's ball of yarn dropped to the floor and rolled a few feet. Edward stooped to retrieve it and held it loosely in his lap, letting slack out as she tugged the yarn. She looked at him, and he smiled, raising his eyebrows. Her dark eyes flashed gladness, then were hidden once more by her lowered lashes. She went on with her knitting, saying nothing but with the faint smile lingering on her lips, and he was content to hold the yarn and watch her.

At last, Mrs. Bowman rose, remarking on the lateness of the hour, and Edward looked to his cousin. Jacob seemed to be making preparations to leave, so Edward rose and offered to carry the tray to the kitchen. His hostess thanked him and went with him to show him where to place it.

When he came back into the front hall, Deborah stood by the stairway alone, and he guessed she had left the parlor to allow Jacob a moment alone with his betrothed. As he approached her, Deborah took a breath and smiled at him a bit shakily.

"Thank you for coming," she said, an unaccustomed crease marring her smooth brow.

"It was a pleasure, and I've thanked your mother for a stimulating evening."

"Discussing wedding plans?" Her doubt colored her tone. "My mother isn't used to entertaining on a large scale, and she's in a dither about this. I'm sure that wasn't the most fascinating conversation you've ever engaged in."

"I don't mind. I shall doubtless see some people there whom I haven't seen in five years or more. Now, if we can only keep Uncle Felix sober that day."

Her eyes widened in alarm, and he bent down to whisper, "Don't worry. Jacob and I have discussed it. We're hiring half a dozen of our strongest men to keep an eye on him the night before and make sure he stays clear of the taverns."

"What about the day of the wedding?"

"Mother won't allow a drop in the house, but even so, I'll detail several men to guard the punch and watch him."

"Thank you. It's not that I don't like him. . . ."

"I know," Edward said. "I like him, too, but I don't entirely trust him in matters of this nature." He reached for her hand, and Deborah turned her eyes upward and looked at him. "I will speak to your father tomorrow. Nothing shall prevent me."

Her lower lip quivered. Then she nodded. "Thank you."

A flood of longing came over him, and he considered for a fleeting moment pulling her into his arms.

No. Not yet.

He smiled and lifted her hand to his lips. "I spoke the truth when I said I enjoyed the evening."

Her luminous smile rewarded him, but at that moment, Abigail and Jacob emerged from the parlor. Abigail's face was flushed, and Edward was satisfied to note that her beauty no longer affected him. A spark of grateful gladness sprang up in his heart as he noted the happiness on his cousin's face.

"Ready to go, Edward?" Jacob asked. "I believe it's still raining, and I thought I'd hail a hack."

"Yes, I'll share with you."

The two young men said good-bye to the ladies, and Edward found himself whistling softly as he and Jacob strolled toward the corner in the drizzle.

"Feeling blithesome tonight, Ed?"

"A bit. And yourself?"

"Euphoric."

"Ah."

They spotted a horse and carriage a short distance down the cross street, and Jacob whistled and waved his hat. The driver pulled the horse around toward them.

"It does my heart good to see you and Abigail so happy," Edward confided when they were in the carriage.

"Thank you. Sometimes I still wonder if you truly don't mind."

"I don't."

Jacob smiled at him in the dim interior of the vehicle. "I'm beginning to believe that. You know, Ed, I never meant to be an interloper."

Edward smiled. "Of course not."

"But I wasn't about to give ground to you, not after. . . Well, my heart was hers already when you came back. Can't undo something like that."

"You can rest easy. I believe God has another future for me."

"Ah, yes. And not an unpleasant one, I think."

"You'll be married in a month," Edward said. "Where will you and Abigail be living afterward?"

"I've something in mind."

"Not with your parents, I hope."

"Oh no," Jacob said quickly. "I couldn't subject Abby to that, although Mother would love to have us there."

"I should say not. Your father scares her."

Jacob gritted his teeth and shrugged. "Not surprising. He scares me sometimes, too."

"Well, I only ask, because. . ." Edward swung round to meet his eyes. "Jacob, Mr. Daniels dropped your salary when I came home."

Jacob opened his mouth, then closed it and fidgeted with his watch fob. "Let's not get into that. I've found a modest house to lease for the next year, and Abigail is agreeable."

"But before I came back, she must have expected something much more lavish."

Jacob shook his head. "It doesn't matter."

"Yes, it does. When we left five years ago, you were first mate on a trading ship. You had the expectation of a nice salary with the firm when you came home and a profit from your private venture."

"So I did."

"But it was nowhere near what you were paid after my father named you his heir apparent."

"Edward!"

"Hear me out. I've looked at the books. I know you were paid considerably more last year than you were before. If Father had left the company to you outright instead of to my mother, you'd own Hunter Shipping now. You'd be taking home what I am now. Instead, I came back and usurped your place."

"I would hardly call it that."

"Fine, but at least admit that on your salary before I disappeared you never could have hoped to support a wife of Abigail's class."

Jacob's face colored. "It's true I'd have thought her beyond my reach in the old days. But—"

"I don't want you and Abby living in a hovel." Suddenly he realized that Jacob must have expected to inherit the Hunter home, too. When Jacob had first proposed to Abigail, he'd probably planned to live with her in the roomy and comfortable house where Edward and his mother lived.

"Really, Ed!" Jacob said. "My salary this past month was cut back to what I earned two years ago, it's true, but it's enough. I'll be able to maintain a respectable household."

"Respectable. Small, plain, not to say stark."

"Yes. And Abigail is not greedy. She understands that things will be a bit more spartan than we'd at first planned. She doesn't care, Edward."

"That's remarkable."

"Isn't it? But it's true. If she did care that much about money, she'd be marrying you instead of me."

Edward took a long, slow breath and sank back. He stared out the window at the dark, wet street and realized they were almost to his aunt and uncle's house.

He was glad Abigail had risen to the occasion and shown her willingness to accept a lower standard of living than she had anticipated. That fit in with the Abigail he remembered. He'd always found her amiable and supportive in the old days. Now she would fulfill that role at Jacob's side.

The driver stopped the hack before the Prices' small clapboard house.

"Look, Jacob, we'll speak more about this later," Edward said. "You've done admirable work for Hunter Shipping, and I expect you'll continue to do so. I doubt I could get along without you now, with the increase in trade we're seeing. With the *Resolute*, our profits will rise, and—well, when it comes right down to it, I'm willing to take less than Father was."

"No, Edward, stop being noble."

"I'm not. I had no idea how much Father drew for a salary. Mother tells me now that he invested much of it, and that kept them going during the war years, when shipping was at a standstill. But so long as Mother is comfortable now, I'd like to see the company pay you a salary that's commensurate with the work you do."

Jacob opened the door of the hack. "Thank you for saying that, but I won't hold you to it. We'll talk again, as you say."

"Fine," said Edward. "Now, quick, before you go, tell me what happened with Captain Stuart."

"They jailed him overnight, but he's engaged an attorney from Boston and is out on bail. I expect he'll be tried when the judge comes here next month."

"And the rest of the crew?"

"Most of the men admitted they knew about it but felt

they had no choice. I'll go over the roster with you tomorrow. There are a few I think we'd be better off without, but most of the fellows are probably all right. However, Mr. Daniels agrees we should prosecute Stuart and Rankin to the fullest."

Edward nodded. "Good. We'll talk about it in the morning." He saw his stocky uncle Felix silhouetted in the doorway of the house, seeming too large for the little dwelling.

"Whattaya doin', wastin' money on a hack?" Felix roared.

"Tell him I'm paying!" Edward called to Jacob through the window.

Jacob turned back and grinned at his cousin. "Been at the ale, I'd say." He faced his father and shouted, "Hush, Father! It's Edward's money. Now, let's get inside."

fifteen

Edward walked from the harbor to Dr. Bowman's surgery the next morning. The small building on Union Street had been erected as a wheelwright's shop, but after the owner's untimely death, the doctor had bought it and refurbished it as a place to attend his patients. He'd kept the wide double door, but instead of wagons and buggies, it now admitted the injured and ill people who sought his services.

Edward entered, pulling off his hat, and looked around. Two women sat stone-faced on a bench near the door, one of them holding a fretful infant. A curtain of linen sheets stitched together stretched across the room, and from behind it, he heard the murmur of voices.

"Is the doctor in?" he asked the older woman, and she nodded toward the curtain.

Edward hesitated, then sat down on the far end of the bench.

A moan came from behind the sheets, followed by Dr. Bowman's hearty, "There, now, that's fine. Just keep the bandage on until you see me again. Come back Friday."

A man in tattered sailor's garb appeared from behind the curtain, holding his left forearm with his other hand. His dirty shirt was stained with blood, and he walked a bit unsteadily. The woman with the baby stood up and walked with him to the door.

A gangly young man who seemed hardly out of his teens poked his head from behind the curtain and looked at the other woman. "Dr. Bowman's ready to see you, mum."

The doctor appeared next, carrying a few instruments and some soiled linen. He dumped the linen into a large basket in the corner and set his tools on a small table, then poured water from a china pitcher into a washbowl and immersed his hands in it.

As he dried his hands, he looked around and saw Edward sitting on the bench.

"Well, lad, this is a surprise. Not ill, I hope."

"No," Edward said, rising. "I only wanted a word with you, sir."

The young man who assisted the doctor was taking fresh linen from a cupboard. Dr. Bowman glanced at the middle-aged woman who was waddling toward the curtained area. "I'll be right with you, Mrs. Atfield."

"I'm next in line, Doctor," she retorted.

"Yes, I'm well aware of that. I shan't be long." He smiled at Edward and whispered, "Here, let's step into my private office."

He opened a door in the side wall, and Edward chuckled, stepping out into a tiny backyard.

"Mrs. Atfield comes at least once a week for her dyspepsia," the doctor said. "It will still be there after we've had our say. How can I help you?"

Edward drew a breath; the tangy salt air seemed inadequate, and he felt a bit lightheaded.

"Sir, I came to ask permission to court your daughter."

Dr. Bowman stared at him, and though Edward feared for a moment he was going to be censured, slowly the man's mouth curved and his eyes began to dance.

"I've heard that from you before."

"Yes, sir, you have. I was sincere then, and I am sincere now."

"Well, since you know I've promised my elder to your cousin, I suppose there's only one conclusion for me to draw."

Edward's smile slipped out of his control. He was sure he looked the buffoon, but he couldn't help it. "Yes, sir. It's Deborah I'd like to court."

"Well, now. Sensible lad." Dr. Bowman slapped him on the

shoulder. "I almost felt the family had taken a grievous loss last month when Abigail chose Jacob. But I see I was early in my conclusion. We get to keep both you boys." He nodded. "I'm pleased. So will Mrs. Bowman be."

"Thank you, sir."

"And I don't have to ask how Debbie feels."

"You don't, sir?"

"No, she's championed your cause from the start."

"That means a lot to me. We've been friends a long time, and I see a staunch loyalty in her, not to mention she's a lovely young woman now."

"Just don't ever let her feel she's your second choice, son."

Edward nodded. "I shall endeavor to let her know that she will be first in my heart from here on."

"Good. Very good." The doctor sighed. "And now I suppose I must get back to Mrs. Atfield. Why don't you join us for dinner this evening?"

"Thank you very much, sir." Edward shook the doctor's hand and watched him go back through the door. He walked around the corner of the building and headed for the harbor, smiling.

He had been thinking on and off for a week about Deborah's charity for sailors' widows, and his mind returned to it as he walked toward the wharves. He'd seen some of the poverty in the shabbier parts of town. Deborah didn't despair about it. She set about to alleviate the worst of it. Through careful inquiries, he'd learned that she not only gave food to those in need, but she also helped the women learn new skills and had even found jobs for a few.

She was like the biblical Ruth, he thought, who gleaned grain for the widowed Naomi. Willing to work hard to help others.

He'd intended to visit the widow of Abijah Crowe, one of the men who fled the *Egret* in the longboat with him and the only one whose family he had not yet contacted. To his surprise, he had heard Deborah mention the name Crowe the day he'd given her the wagonload of provisions, and now he wanted to learn whether Abijah Crowe's wife was one of the women to whom Deborah ministered. He decided the staff at Hunter Shipping would not miss him if he stayed away another hour.

He recalled the directions Deborah had given the day she collected her goods at the warehouse. By asking about in the neighborhood, he soon found the Crowe house. The humble cottage looked in need of repair; however, the front stoop was neat, and bright curtains hung at the window that faced the street. He knocked, wishing he had dressed differently—not in the tailed coat he wore to the office most days. But it was too late. The door creaked open, and he looked into the face of a thin woman with dull, brown hair. Her cheeks were hollow and her hands bony.

"Hello," he said.

"What do you want?" Her eyes narrowed as she looked him over.

"Mrs. Crowe?"

"I be her."

"I'm Edward Hunter."

She stared at him blankly, and he thought she did not recognize the name.

He said, "I heard your name mentioned by Miss Bowman. Deborah Bowman."

The woman drew her shoulders back and scowled at him. "And?"

"Well, I wondered if you were possibly related to Abijah Crowe."

Her gaze pierced him, and he stared back.

"He were my late husband."

Edward sighed. "I was with Abijah on the *Egret*."

"I know it. I heared you came back after all this time."

He nodded. "After our ship sank, Abijah was with me and a

few others in the ship's longboat."

She said nothing but continued to watch him, unblinking.

"I. . .meant to come and visit you earlier. I've tried to visit the families of all the men who were in my boat."

"Nancy Webber told me you came to see her."

"Yes. Her John and I were together on the island for quite some time, and we got along well. I was glad I could tell her what her husband meant to me in those days." Edward removed his hat and wiped the perspiration from his brow. It was nearing noon, and the sun's rays made him uncomfortably warm.

"Do you want to set a spell?" she asked.

"I should be glad to if you've no objection."

Mrs. Crowe turned and shuffled into the cottage, and he followed. Two children about five and seven years old scuttled out of the way and tumbled onto a bunk, where they crouched and stared at him.

Edward took the stool the woman indicated near the cold hearth, and she sat opposite him.

"Thought you weren't going to come here," she said.

"I'm sorry I put it off, ma'am. It took me awhile to get used to being home again, and I've been back at work the past few weeks. But I believe I've gotten round to all the other families. I'm sorry it took me so long to find you."

She nodded once and reached behind her for a ball of yarn and a carved wooden hook. As she began to crochet, Edward studied the yarn. It looked very familiar.

"My Abijah died in that boat," she said.

"Yes, ma'am, he did. I'm sorry. He was a good man and a good sailor."

She frowned but kept on hooking the yarn through the endless loops.

"He spoke of you and the children."

Her hands stilled, and she sniffed. "What did he say?"

"He asked the captain, at the end, to remember him to

you. And he said he didn't want the children to grow up fatherless."

"The captain died, too," she said, not looking at him.

"Yes, ma'am, he did. Several days later. But I tried to remember all the messages the men had given him in case I ever made it home."

"How did he die?"

"Abijah?" Edward asked.

She nodded.

"I'm afraid it was lack of water, ma'am. We started out with very little, and we all suffered from it."

"It's a terrible death." Her ball of yarn dropped from her lap and skittered across the floor, and Edward jumped to catch it.

He took it back to Mrs. Crowe and handed it to her. "Deborah Bowman brought you this yarn."

Her eyebrows drew together. "You're the man who owned the ship. The man Miss Abigail was going to marry."

"You know her?"

"Surely. She comes here with her sister and helps with the sewing and tells stories to the kiddies."

He sat down again. "My father owned the *Egret*. And yes, I was betrothed to Abigail Bowman when I left here five years ago."

"But she found some other fellow she liked more." She shook her head. "I thought better of her than that."

Edward cleared his throat. "It wasn't quite like that, Mrs. Crowe. You see, my cousin was also on the ship with your husband and me, but when the *Egret* went down, he was in the other boat. His boat was picked up, and my cousin Mr. Price came home thinking I was dead. After several years of believing I had perished, Miss Bowman agreed to marry Mr. Price."

"She shouldn't, though. Not now that you're here."

"Well, I thought so myself at first, but God has shown me a better plan."

"A better plan?"

"Yes. I believe our heavenly Father brought them together in their grief and that He has another woman chosen to be my wife."

"Oh?" She looked doubtful, and he smiled.

"Yes, ma'am. This morning, I've been making arrangements to call upon another young lady. Someone I think you'd approve of."

"I?"

He nodded.

"Not Miss Debbie?"

"Yes."

Mrs. Crowe began to smile at last. "She be a fine young lady."

"Indeed she is."

"She gets victuals for those as can't buy them, and she sews togs for the little ones. She even brought me fine cotton for curtains." The woman nodded toward her small window, and Edward turned to observe the red calico fabric that hung there.

He smiled at her. "She told me that she had friends down here."

Mrs. Crowe's chin came up several inches. "She does. And she ain't ashamed to claim them. Miss Debbie says anyone who believes in Jesus is her sister."

Edward nodded. He could almost hear her saying that. "I'm so glad she is your friend, and I wanted to bring you something." He reached into his coat pocket and brought out a small pouch of coins. "Mrs. Crowe, Hunter Shipping has made a gift to the family of each man who died when the *Egret* sank."

"Don't want no gifts."

"But, ma'am, your husband served the company well."

"Don't need no charity. Now Miss Debbie, she comes down here, she shares with us, and she sits and stitches with us. She shows us how to do things. She taught me to spin raw wool, she did. The food she brings is for them that's starving. This family's not starving."

"I'm glad to hear that. How do you live, ma'am?"

"My older son, John, goes out with Abe Fuller fishing every day, and Thomas, the next one down, he runs errands for the haberdasher and the butcher, and sometimes Captain Moody. We get by."

"That's commendable. I'm glad your sons are able to work. But this money that I've brought you isn't charity. It's coming to you for your husband's good service. He did his job on the *Egret* until the day she foundered, and if he'd made it home, he'd have been paid for every day of that work. Hunter Shipping owes your husband money, Mrs. Crowe. But since he's not here to receive it, I would like to give it to his heirs, meaning you and the children. It's the pay he would have gotten for the days he worked, not a penny more."

She pursed her lips together. "My man was a good man."

"Yes he was." Edward set the little pouch on the table near her, and she did not protest.

"You say he died in that boat before the captain died."

"Yes." Edward rubbed a hand across his forehead. The harsh memories deluged him once more, and he sent up a silent prayer for peace. "We were in the boat for a fortnight, ma'am. Your husband lasted ten days, I believe. Longer than a couple of the others."

"Was he in distress?" she whispered.

"We all were. I won't lie to you, ma'am. It was awful."

She nodded. "And he's buried at sea?"

"Yes, ma'am." He reached into his pocket again. "I believe this was his." He held out a small knife he had removed from Abijah Crowe's pocket before they lowered him over the side of the boat. "I used it during my time on the island and was thankful to have it. Very useful it was. In fact, I might not be alive now if it weren't for this. But now. . .well, I thought your older boy might like to have it."

She took the knife in her hand and stared down at it. It was a poorly forged blade with a handle of deer's antler. Tears welled in her eyes and spilled down her cheeks. " 'Twas Abijah's all right. Thank you."

Edward left after wishing her well. He walked along the shore, surveying the wharves and boats without seeing them. After ten minutes, he stopped, realizing he had come to Hunter's Wharf. Instead of heading across the street to the office, he walked all the way to the end of the wharf, past several moored vessels and the shops and chandlery. At the end of the wharf, he halted and stood gazing down into the water that swirled around the massive pilings.

At last his duty to the families was concluded, though he knew he would have dealings with many of them again. Amos Mitchell's son was now his employee. He prayed he would never have to face Mrs. Mitchell again on such an errand.

He recalled Mrs. Crowe's face as she looked down at her dead husband's knife. He'd seen similar reactions when he had delivered mementos to other families. The captain's wife had accepted his compass and quadrant with dignity, but even so, her face had crumpled as she examined the items. Davy Wilkes hadn't had anything in his pockets, and Edward had sliced a button from his coat before they eased his body overboard. His mother had wept over that, saying she'd stitched it to his woolen coat a few days before he'd sailed.

For Gideon Bramwell's parents, he'd delivered the key the boy wore on a thong around his neck. Edward had thought it belonged to Gideon's sea chest, which was now in the bottom of the ocean, but his mother told him it belonged to the chest that the girl he loved had filled with household items and vowed never to open until he returned with the key.

For each one of the seven men in the boat with him, he'd managed to preserve some small item to convey back to their families. John Webber had carved a wooden chain from a piece of driftwood he found on the island. It was more than two feet long when he died. Edward had chopped off the excess wood and carried the chain home to Mrs. Webber. With Amos Mitchell, who was lost out of the small boat in high seas, Edward had only a misshapen hat left behind where he'd sat. For Isaac Towers, they'd found pinned inside his pocket a small emerald brooch he'd bought in Rio and was planning to take home to his wife.

What would they have brought home if it were me? Edward wondered. The trinkets he'd bought for Abigail and his mother were sunk and gone. His clothes had gone to rags, and the few tools he'd had on the island had belonged to others. In his excitement on being rescued, he'd brought only the grass pouch he'd woven to hold the mementos of the men. Just one other thing had made it home with him from the long adventure. He shoved his hand in his pocket and rubbed his thumb over the smooth, rounded shell he'd carried for several months now. He'd stooped to pick it from the sand one morning, and when he straightened and glanced toward the sea, there, incredibly, was a ship under sail, making for his island. His ordeal was over. He had thrust the smooth shell into his pocket and run toward the surf, shouting and waving his arms. His isolation had ended.

He closed his eyes and inhaled the salty air, feeling the breeze on his face and the sun on his shoulders. It didn't matter that he'd lost all. What mattered was the way he handled what God had given back to him.

"Thank You, dear Father, for bringing me home. Use me in what is left of my life as You see fit."

Finally he opened his eyes and turned toward his office.

sixteen

Deborah's heart soared as she opened the front door to Edward.

I have the right to love him now. Thank You, Lord.

The answering light in Edward's eyes sent anticipation surging through her. Modesty said she should avert her gaze, but she couldn't look away. Instead, she smiled and reached for his hand, drawing him into the house.

"I'm so glad you're here. Abby is dining with the Price family tonight, but Father and Mother are eager to see you."

She led him to the dining room, where her parents greeted him.

"You see, I tore myself away from my patients this evening," Dr. Bowman said.

"I'm delighted, sir." Edward shook his hand and turned to his wife. "Thank you for your kind invitation, Mrs. Bowman."

"We're pleased you could come. Sit here, Edward, where Abigail usually sits. Jacob has carried her off to spend the evening with his family tonight."

A thin, sober-faced woman served them under gentle instruction from Mrs. Bowman. When the maid carried the platter of lamb in and set it before the doctor, her hands shook so that the china hit the table with a loud *clunk*, and the woman jumped, flushing to the roots of her hair.

"There, now," said Dr. Bowman. "A nice leg of lamb. Thank you, Mrs. . . . What's the name again?" He looked around vaguely toward his wife.

"It's Mrs. Rafferty, Father," Deborah said.

"Ah, yes. And is there sauce?"

"Aye, sir." The woman curtsied and dashed for the kitchen.

"Mrs. Rafferty is a friend of mine," Deborah said to Edward, hoping he would understand that she meant one of her Thursday widows. "She told me that she hopes to earn a bit of money in service, so Mother agreed to train her."

"If she works out well, I may recommend her to your mother, Edward." Mrs. Bowman raised her eyebrows. "Has she found a replacement for Jenny Hapworth yet?"

"No, she hasn't. I'm sure she'd be happy to consider anyone you vouch for."

"She's green, but she's willing to learn."

Deborah smiled at him. "We have Elizabeth in during the day, but because Mother has no one to help serve dinner, we've been letting Mrs. Rafferty practice on us this week. Usually one of us helps her, but I think she's doing splendidly, don't you?"

At that moment, the maid cautiously pushed the door open and entered, bearing a steaming dish and a pewter ladle on a tray. She inched toward Dr. Bowman's end of the table and set the tray down with a sigh.

"Thank you," he said, reaching for the gravy.

Mrs. Rafferty dipped her head, then looked toward Mrs. Bowman.

"Perhaps Mr. Hunter would like more potatoes?" the mistress suggested.

"Oh no, ma'am, I'm fine," Edward assured her. "I don't eat as much as I used to."

"Short rations for a long spell will do that to you," the doctor said.

"But it's delicious," Edward said quickly, and Deborah smiled at him. "The biscuits are very light, too. Much like my mother's."

Deborah said nothing but knew her face was beaming. Mrs. Hunter had watched her bake twenty batches of biscuits one rainy day until Deborah's were identical to her own. The children of the fishermen's shacks had reaped the bounty of her cooking lesson, with their fill of biscuits delivered and distributed by Mrs. Hunter's gardener.

But her mother was not about to ignore a chance to brag about her talented daughter.

"Deborah made the biscuits, and aren't they flavorful? She baked the pie you'll be enjoying later as well."

Edward sent a look across the table that topped approval. Deborah could only interpret it as thorough admiration, and she whipped her napkin up to hide the silly grin that stretched across her face.

Her father began once more to ask Edward about his travels, and Edward obliged by recounting tales of the sea and the ports he had visited. Deborah listened, enthralled. What would it be like to travel to such strange places? She was sure her imagination was inadequate to show her the wonders Edward described.

"Are you happier on dry land?" Mrs. Bowman asked.

"In some ways." Edward reached for his water glass and shot Deborah a smile.

"Jacob says he'll stay ashore now," Dr. Bowman asserted. "I'm afraid Abby's making a landlubber out of him."

"There, now, that's all right," said his wife. "Jacob says one shipwreck was enough for him, and he doesn't mind not sailing anymore."

"We've plenty to keep him busy at the office," Edward said. "I doubt I would undertake any long Pacific voyages again, but I might take one of our company schooners to the West Indies."

"That's a profitable destination for you, is it not?" The doctor carved a second helping of lamb for himself.

"It's the backbone of our trade. The goods are perhaps not as exotic or expensive, but we can make more trips there and back."

"Volume," Dr. Bowman agreed.

When the meal was over, Mrs. Rafferty brought the coffee tray to the parlor, where Mrs. Bowman poured and the doctor continued the discussion with Edward about trading and the outlook of Hunter Shipping. Deborah felt sure he was pumping her caller about his financial prospects, and perhaps Jacob's as well, but Edward didn't seem to mind.

At last, Mrs. Bowman rose. "I must see Mrs. Rafferty before she leaves for the night. And, my dear, you said you would get a hack to drive her home."

Dr. Bowman took his cue and stood as well. "Yes, she can't walk all that way alone after dark. There, Edward, I've kept you rambling on about business all evening. I expect you young folks have other subjects to discuss."

Edward had jumped up when his hostess stood, and once more he shook hands with the doctor.

"Thank you for having me in, sir."

Her father laughed. "I expect I shall be seeing a lot more of you. Come around my little surgery anytime you wish to talk, Edward."

"Thank you. I will."

"And don't keep Deborah up too late."

"No, sir."

Edward watched the parents leave the room, then looked down at Deborah and took a deep breath.

"It seems I am to be trusted now without a chaperone."

She nodded. "You do seem to be well favored."

"Would it be too forward of me to sit beside you?"

She felt her throat tingle and swallowed hard, then managed to say, "Not at all."

He came around to the sofa and sat on the cushion next to her, suddenly very close, and Deborah's stomach fluttered.

"You haven't said much this evening."

She smiled at that. "Well, you know Father. When he gets onto a topic, he won't let go."

Edward nodded. "I saw him this morning."

She stared at the fire screen that covered the empty fireplace. "I thought you must have."

They sat in silence for a moment, and she wondered if she ought to ask the outcome of that encounter.

"He. . .seemed a little sad at the thought of an empty house," Edward said.

"A what?" She stared at him, at his rich brown eyes and the dear, disorderly lock of hair that fell over his forehead.

"Well, if both his daughters left home, I mean."

She turned away, but it was too late. The telltale blush had returned, though she'd determined not to let it.

He grasped her hand lightly, and joy shot through her.

"I don't expect they'll go so far away that they can't visit," she whispered.

"I seem to recall you saying you'd like to sail one day."

She nodded. "So I should."

"I know you'd love it. But I wouldn't entrust you to just any ship or any captain."

Feeling very daring, she said, "And to whom would you entrust me?"

"I believe the *Resolute* will make trade voyages to the Indies soon."

"How soon?"

"Well, Mr. Price, the second officer of Hunter Shipping, tells me she'll sail within the month under Captain Redding. But this winter, that is, after the hurricane season. . ."

Deborah found enough courage to look up into his face once more.

Edward smiled and lifted a hand to her cheek. His voice cracked as he continued. "Mr. Price tells me that she'll sail again then under a different master."

"Oh?"

"Yes."

"As you say, I shouldn't want to go with just anyone."

"By then the company thinks it can spare its owner for a few months, and the ship will sail under. . .Captain Hunter."

Deborah took two deep breaths, trying to calm her raging

pulse before answering. "I hear he comes from one of the oldest Maine families and a long line of sea captains and ship owners."

"I've heard that, too. Farmers of the oldest stock turned sailors."

She felt his arm warm around her shoulders, and he eased toward her. A flash of panic struck her but then was gone. She had nothing to fear with Edward. She surrendered and leaned her head against his chest, where his broadcloth jacket parted to show his snowy linen shirt. With a deep sigh, he folded her in his embrace and laid his cheek on top of her head. She heard his heart beating as fast as hers.

"Deborah?"

"Yes?"

"I love you."

"And I've always loved you."

He tilted her chin up and searched her eyes for a moment, and her heart tripped as their gazes met. He bent to kiss her, and she luxuriated in the moment, resting in his arms.

"Can you forget the past?" he whispered.

"I doubt it. Not altogether. But we learn from the past."

"Yes."

He was silent, holding her close to his heart and stroking her hair. "I shall always love you," he said.

"And I you."

He pushed away and fumbled in his coat pocket. When he brought his hand out, a round, brown-speckled shell rested in his palm.

"What is it?" she asked. "I've never seen one like it."

"It's all I have from the island. The few other things we had, I gave to the men's families for remembrances. But I'd like to give you this."

She took it and ran a finger over its hard, satiny curve. "Thank you."

"And I hope we'll sail together one day and find other mementos."

He went to one knee beside her and clasped her hands, with the shell hidden between her palm and his.

"I'd like to bring you another keepsake soon. A ring, dearest. Will you be my wife?"

Deborah caught her breath. Would her father object and say it was too soon?

A certainty overcame her misgivings. This was what she had waited for these many years. This was why she had reserved her heart from loving any others.

"Yes," she whispered. "I shall be honored."

He drew her toward him and kissed her once more, and Deborah knew her own solitude had ended, too.

epilogue

A cool October breeze blew in off Casco Bay and ruffled the limbs of the trees around them. A tall maple waved its branches, and red and yellow leaves fluttered down into the Hunters' garden. Edward seized Deborah's hand, and she smiled at him, then looked down and waved at the people below.

They were mad to get married on the tiny rooftop platform, but this was Deborah's choice. Indian summer had hit the Maine coast, and she had reveled in the warm, clear autumn days the last two weeks had brought. Edward had agreed to her suggestion for the wedding venue as he agreed to nearly everything she asked, eager to please her in the tiniest detail. Still, it was a bit cooler today, and harsh weather was not far away.

The two of them, Pastor Jordan, their witnesses and parents were all the widow's walk could hold. The other guests filled the garden and spilled over onto the walk. A few of Deborah's Thursday ladies and their children even stood outside the neat white fence, gazing up at them with awe.

Jacob and Abigail joined them at the railing. Edward's mother and Dr. and Mrs. Bowman left the shelter of the stairway and came to stand beside them. Mrs. Hunter was swathed in a fur cape and a woolen hood, but still, Edward hoped the ceremony would be short.

"Perhaps this wasn't such a good idea," Abigail said to her sister.

"I'm sorry. Are you cold?" Deborah asked.

"A bit."

Jacob seemed to feel this was license to slip his arm around his wife of two months and hold her close to his side, and Edward winked at him.

"Let us begin," said the pastor. "Dearly beloved, we are gathered here in this unusual place. . . ."

They all chuckled, and the pastor went on with the timeless words.

Edward pulled Deborah's hand through the crook of his arm and held it firmly as they recited their vows.

As the ritual ended, they bowed their heads, and the pastor invoked God's blessing.

"You may kiss the bride."

Edward leaned down to kiss Deborah tenderly. He felt the change in wind as it rippled his hair and sent his necktie fluttering to the side. When they separated, he opened his eyes and automatically sought the observatory tower.

"A ship!"

"Hush, Edward," said Abigail. "This is your wedding day. Stop looking up there."

"You mustn't be thinking of business," Jacob agreed.

"But a ship is heading for our wharf, and it can't be one of ours."

Jacob squinted toward the fluttering signal.

"Spanish."

"You sure?" Edward frowned, wishing he had the spyglass.

"Don't worry," Jacob said. "My father's in the warehouse. He insisted on working today on the odds something like this would happen. He and the harbor master will see to it."

Their parents stepped forward to embrace them.

"Come in out of the wind," Mrs. Hunter said, leading the way to the door. "I'll have Hannah open the front door for our guests. We're serving in the double parlor, not the yard."

"I'm sorry it turned too chilly to eat outside," Deborah said, making her way cautiously down the steep attic stairs behind her mother-in-law.

"Don't fret," Mrs. Hunter replied. "I've planned on it all

along. Can't trust the weather in these parts. But I'm glad you didn't plan dancing on the wharf, Deborah."

"Dancing on the wharf?" Abigail asked as they reached the hallway below. "What a novel idea."

Edward smiled and squeezed Deborah's hand. He'd have gone along with it if Deborah had wanted it, but she'd confided that her mother would find it too raucous, and it was just as well. It would have been chaos with a foreign ship landing during the reception for the newlyweds.

The parlor was already filled with distinguished guests. Governor and Mrs. King and the state's congressmen rubbed elbows with ship owners, merchants, and Dr. Bowman's patients. Edward's sister, Anne, greeted the couple with a radiant smile, and her husband brought their two little ones over to kiss their new aunt. Deborah's widowed friends hung back in the yard, too timid to enter at first, but Edward took his bride out to stand on the front porch and urge them inside, along with most of the men employed by Hunter Shipping, where he had declared a half holiday.

"We shall cut the cake in a moment." Deborah's eyes glowed as she hugged Mrs. Crowe. "Hannah Rafferty helped Mrs. Hunter bake it, and you must have a piece. All the children, too."

The ladies came inside at last, with downcast eyes, peeking up now and then at their opulent surroundings. Abigail went around with a basket of little bags of sweets, handing one to each child. The rooms were crowded, but Edward stationed himself at Deborah's side, knowing she was determined to speak to each guest. She greeted each poor widow as graciously as she did the congressmen's wives.

At last, the guests began to slip away, and only the newlyweds' families were left.

Felix Price entered, filling the doorway with his bulk.

"Any cake left?" he roared.

"Yes, Father," Jacob told him. "We fed near a hundred

people, but even so, I think we'll be eating cake for a week."

Aunt Ruth hurried to fix a plate for him, and Felix sought Edward out.

"Well, now, there ye be with your beautiful bride."

Deborah smiled up at him. "Thank you, Mr. Price. It was kind of you to tend to business while Edward and Jacob were otherwise occupied."

"You're welcome, lass. But you must call me Uncle." He glanced at Edward. "May I kiss the bride?"

Before he could respond, Deborah turned her cheek to Felix, and he planted a loud smack on it, then turned to Edward with a grin.

"It's a fine Spanish brigantine at your wharf this minute."

"What's in her hold?" Edward asked.

"Olives and their oil, sugar, grain, wheat, and oranges."

"Oranges?"

"Aye. They look to be all right. A few spoiled, but I think they picked them green."

Jacob shook his head. "We'll have to have market day tomorrow. I'll send word around to all the buyers."

"Half of them were here today," Edward said. "If we'd known half an hour ago, we could have told them all at once. But you're right; unload as soon as possible. Most of it will keep well, but the fruit has to be sold quickly."

"There's cork, too," Felix added. "Big bundles of it."

"Good, we can sell that for certain." Jacob extended his hand to Edward. "Sounds like I should get down to the wharf. Abby can go home with her parents. Don't worry, Edward, we'll turn a good profit on this cargo."

"Should I come down in the morning?" Edward asked, glancing at Deborah. She closed her lips tight but made no objection.

"Of course not!" Jacob glared at him as though he had uttered heresy. "You have two weeks' honeymoon before you and Deborah sail in the *Resolute*. And you are not to show your face at the office during that time."

Deborah laughed. "Oh, please, Jacob. If you think you can keep him away for two weeks, you're daft. Besides, we'll be going back and forth to the *Resolute* while you're loading her. I expect you might see both of us once or twice during the interval."

"Yes," Edward said, patting her hand. "I insisted Deborah decorate the cabin for her comfort and bring along plenty of clothing. We'll be making a few trips to bring our baggage to the ship and get things settled."

"Fine." Jacob stepped back, looking around the room and smiling when his gaze lit on Abby. "Just don't let me see you for a few days at least, Ed. You'll scandalize the clerks if you show your face within a week."

Felix roared with laughter as his wife approached with a plate of food and a glass of punch. Edward noted Deborah's scarlet cheeks and guided her into the hallway, then, seeing they hadn't been followed, up the stairs and into the room his mother had designated as Deborah's new sitting room. The chamber adjoined the large bedchamber they would share and was fitted out with delicate cherry furniture and bright hangings and cushions.

"Are you tired?" he asked. "I thought you might want to sit for a moment, here where it's quiet."

"No, I'm not tired, but I'm glad to have a minute in private with my husband."

He swept her into his arms, blocking from his mind the preparations, the ceremony, the chitchat with the guests. This was his reward for long patience. This exhilarating moment brought him such joy that he could not speak but held her tight, brushing his cheek against her silky hair and inhaling her scent.

"Hasn't it been a splendid day?" she whispered.

"Perfect."

He kissed her then as he had longed to kiss her for months

now, prolonging the interlude and relishing the light pressure of her arms as they slid around him.

When he at last released her, she nestled in against his vest, and he cradled her there.

"You know," he murmured, "I never thought I'd want to go back to Spring Island, but now I'm thinking it wouldn't be so bad, if you were there with me."

She laughed and squeezed him. "If you want to be marooned again, Edward, and live a wild life as a castaway, that's fine with me. Just do take me with you."

"No fear." He stroked her soft, dark hair and kissed her brow. "I shan't let you out of my sight now that I've found you."

A Letter To Our Readers

Dear Reader:
In order that we might better contribute to your reading enjoyment, we would appreciate your taking a few minutes to respond to the following questions. We welcome your comments and read each form and letter we receive. When completed, please return to the following:

Fiction Editor
Heartsong Presents
PO Box 719
Uhrichsville, Ohio 44683

1. Did you enjoy reading *The Castaway's Bride* by Susan Page Davis?
   ❏ Very much! I would like to see more books by this author!
   ❏ Moderately. I would have enjoyed it more if

   _____

   _____

   _____

2. Are you a member of **Heartsong Presents**? ❏ Yes ❏ No
   If no, where did you purchase this book? _____

   _____

3. How would you rate, on a scale from 1 (poor) to 5 (superior), the cover design? _____

4. On a scale from 1 (poor) to 10 (superior), please rate the following elements.

   ____ Heroine   ____ Plot
   ____ Hero   ____ Inspirational theme
   ____ Setting   ____ Secondary characters

5. These characters were special because? _____
   _____
   _____

6. How has this book inspired your life? _____
   _____
   _____

7. What settings would you like to see covered in future
   Heartsong Presents books? _____
   _____
   _____

8. What are some inspirational themes you would like to see
   treated in future books? _____
   _____
   _____

9. Would you be interested in reading other **Heartsong
   Presents** titles? ❑ Yes ❑ No

10. Please check your age range:
    ❑ Under 18   ❑ 18-24
    ❑ 25-34   ❑ 35-45
    ❑ 46-55   ❑ Over 55

Name _____
Occupation _____
Address _____
City, State, Zip _____

LOVE LETTERS

4 stories in 1

Women looking for relief from their difficult life situations find comfort and freedom through the written word. Whether it's through a song, a fortune cookie, a Post-It Note, or an e-mail, their paths lead them to a greater peace and ultimately love.

Four beautiful stories of women who find love by authors Mary Davis, Kathleen K. Kovach, Sally Laity, and Jeri Odell.

Historical, paperback, 352 pages, 5³/₁₆" x 8"